Emily Harvale lives in Ea
although she would prefe
Alps…or Canada…or anywhere that has several
months of snow. Emily loves snow almost as much
as she loves Christmas.

Having worked in the City (London) for several
years, Emily returned to her home town of
Hastings where she spends her days writing. And
wondering if it will snow.

You can contact her via her website, Twitter,
Facebook or Instagram.

There is also a Facebook group where fans can
chat with Emily about her books, her writing day
and life in general. Details are on the 'For You'
page of Emily's website.

Author contacts:
www.emilyharvale.com
www.twitter.com/emilyharvale
www.facebook.com/emilyharvalewriter
www.instagram.com/emilyharvale

***

Scan the code above to see all Emily's books on Amazon

Also by this author

Highland Fling
Lizzie Marshall's Wedding
The Golf Widows' Club
Sailing Solo
Carole Singer's Christmas
Christmas Wishes
A Slippery Slope
The Perfect Christmas Plan
Be Mine
It Takes Two
Bells and Bows on Mistletoe Row

The Goldebury Bay series:
Ninety Days of Summer – book 1
Ninety Steps to Summerhill – book 2
Ninety Days to Christmas – book 3

The Hideaway Down series:
A Christmas Hideaway – book 1
Catch A Falling Star – book 2
Walking on Sunshine – book 3
Dancing in the Rain – book 4

Hall's Cross series
Deck the Halls – book 1
The Starlight Ball – book 2

Michaelmas Bay series
Christmas Secrets in Snowflake Cove – book 1
Blame it on the Moonlight – book 2

Lily Pond Lane series
The Cottage on Lily Pond Lane –
Part One – New beginnings and Summer secrets
Part Two – Autumn leaves and Trick or treat
Christmas on Lily Pond Lane
Return to Lily Pond Lane
A Wedding on Lily Pond Lane

Return

to

Lily Pond Lane

Emily Harvale

ISBN 978-1-909917-41-5

Published by Crescent Gate Publishing

Print edition published worldwide 2019
E-edition published worldwide 2019

Editor Christina Harkness

Cover design by JR and Emily Harvale

To the wonderful members of my Facebook group,
Emily Harvale's Readers' Club.
You help me far more than you realise. Thank you
for your support, friendship and wisdom and for
making me smile on the days when I'm struggling
to believe in myself. You're the best!

Acknowledgements

My grateful thanks go to the following:

Christina Harkness for her patience and care in editing this book.
My webmaster, David Cleworth who does so much more than website stuff.
My cover design team, JR.
Luke Brabants. Luke is a talented artist and can be found at: www.lukebrabants.com
My wonderful friends for their friendship and love. You know I love you all.
All the fabulous members of my Readers' Club. You help and support me in so many ways and I am truly grateful for your ongoing friendship. I wouldn't be where I am today without you.
My Twitter and Facebook friends, and fans of my Facebook author page. It's great to chat with you. You help to keep me (relatively) sane!
Thank you for buying this book.

Return

To

Lily Pond Lane

Chapter One

Mia flicked on the switch and momentarily closed her eyes against the glare; the lights in the kitchen of Little Pond Farm were substantially brighter than in the capacious hall. She padded across the floor, her slippers slapping on the tiles, her mouth wide open in a yawn and caught a glimpse of herself in the window opposite, her image distorted in the six over six, Georgian panes. Her golden brown hair, which had been tied in a loose bun before she went to bed now bore a remarkable likeness to a bird nest about to fall from its perch. But after such a restless night, followed by a good – no, scratch that – by a fantastic hour or so of sex and general fooling around with Jet, that was no surprise. She pulled at the scrunchy for a couple of seconds and tucked several locks of hair back in place. Not that it made much difference.

Despite the central heating being on full pelt and with the certain knowledge that Jet would have refuelled the Range, the air in the spacious kitchen was a little chilly and she tugged the haphazardly tied, luxurious, purple fleece dressing gown more tightly around her. It was one of the presents Jet had bought her for Christmas. She had been a bit surprised at the time when she'd opened the beautifully wrapped box and seen it. Thick fleece dressing gowns didn't exactly scream, 'young, sexy, vibrant woman,' did they? They were more the sort of thing her mum might wear. Or more likely, Hettie Turner. Jet must have read her mind because he'd given her one of his disarmingly devilish grins and said: 'Sexy, huh? I was tempted to buy you something short and see-through, but because I love you so much, I bought you this. I want you to be warm, not freeze to death. Besides,' he had added with a wink, 'you look sexy in everything.'

On a freezing cold morning such as this, she was glad of it. Little Pond Farm might be a perfect example of a Georgian farmhouse, but the massive doors and original glass windows let an inordinate amount of draughts into the high-ceilinged rooms. Added to which, the farmhouse was perched on top of a hill at the end of a long drive. The 360-degree views were breathtaking, but at this time of year so were the winter winds that blew from the north and the gales from the south-west which swept in from the sea less than a mile away. And at seven-thirty in the morning, Mia wasn't the only one apparently struggling to wake up. The sun seemed reluctant to show its face, despite the forecast promising a sunny day for the first time in at least a week. Still half-asleep, Mia filled the kettle and switched it on before resting her arms on the worktop and closing her tired eyes.

She had hardly slept a wink. Vivid dreams had tormented her and she tossed and turned so often that she even woke Jet a couple of times. Which took some doing. The man made the proverbial log look restless. It astonished her how soundly he could sleep. Usually.

Once or twice since she had officially moved in with him at Christmas, she had resorted to jabbing him with her finger to make sure he was still breathing, only reassured when a tiny sigh or the softest snore escaped him. It was foolish of course. Jet was fit – in every sense of the word, but her best friend, Ella had shown her an article about people dying in their sleep and … well, it was better to be safe than sorry.

Last night though, Jet hadn't got much more sleep than Mia. Each time she screamed, or cried herself awake, he woke up too and held her in his arms to comfort her, switching on his bedside lamp as if the golden glow it gave might help to combat her fear.

'It's just a nightmare, Mia.' His voice croaky from sleep and he had given a small cough to clear his throat. 'Try to go back to sleep. You're safe. I'm here.'

She was safe. She knew that. But every time she went back to sleep, the dream returned. The worst part was she could not recall what it was about. She simply woke with a start and a heavy feeling of despondency and doom, or with tears trickling down her cheeks and the unshakeable certainty that something terrible was going to happen.

'Perhaps it's a premonition.' She wriggled closer to Jet's warm, firm body to assuage her fears. 'I can't remember what I dreamt but I know it wasn't good.'

He kissed her on the top of her head as he held her in a tender embrace. 'Perhaps it's too much blue cheese for supper,' he joked, stroking her cheek reassuringly. 'You've eaten it for the last two nights in a row. Didn't Hettie say something over Christmas about never having cheese before bed because it gives you bad dreams?' He kissed her again, this time on the tip of her nose. 'But nothing bad's going to happen, Mia. The future's looking bright.'

Mia nodded her head against his neck. He was right. Both about what Hettie had said and about the future looking bright. It did. Especially so since he had proposed to her on Christmas morning.

She was the luckiest girl in the world.

So why was she suddenly feeling anxious? She had nothing to be worried about. The man she adored felt the same way about her. She had fabulous friends and a wonderful mum. She was rich. She was healthy. Possibly not quite as healthy as she should be but certainly more so than when she had first arrived in Little Pondale. No more microwave meals, or ding-dinners as Ella called them, for her. Definitely no take-aways, although that was partly due to the fact that the nearest Indian or Chinese were a good thirty minutes away. Hardly any pizzas either, unless they were made from scratch. Now that she was learning to cook, she had become far more food-conscious. Sourcing fresh, local ingredients was not only good for her, it was fun.

Life was great. She had everything. The future wasn't merely bright; it was blindingly brilliant.

Mia glanced up at Jet. Yep. She really was the luckiest girl in the world. Apart from being gorgeous, Jet Cross was kind and caring – not to mention, pretty sensational in bed. She still had to pinch herself sometimes to believe all this was really happening. Inheriting a fortune from her great-aunt Mattie, whom Mia hadn't even known existed less than a year ago; moving to Little Pondale, along with her best friend Ella and Ella's twin brother, Garrick; meeting Jet and, after a few wrong turns, falling head over heels in love with him; getting engaged and moving in with him just two months after their first real date. This was the stuff of fairy tales.

'I know,' she said. 'Perhaps that's the problem. I don't mean it's a problem that things are going so well. I mean it's all going far too well. And not just for us.'

'I don't think many people would see that as a problem, Mia. Most people would thank their lucky stars and make the most of it.'

'Maybe. But think about it. In less than a year we fell madly in love, are living together and engaged. My mum fell head over heels in love with Franklin, a man half her age, and is now living with him in one of your farm cottages. Ella and Gill are besotted with each other and I don't think it'll be long before he pops the question. Although I bet you anything, Ella will laugh when they're standing at the altar and the vicar uses Gill's full name. "Do you, Ella Swann take Guillaume De Fonteneau to be your lawfully wedded husband?" Mind you, that's better than her laughing when she tells everyone to pronounce Gill, like a fish gill and not like Jill because he's not a girl.' Mia shook her head and grinned, almost hearing her friend's voice as she spoke, before continuing: 'And … Hettie met Fred and they're blissfully happy since their whirlwind wedding last autumn. Jenny moved from Florence to take over her cousin's bakery, changed the name to Lake's Bakes and made it even more successful than it was when Justin owned it. Glen came here on a temporary basis, was swept off his feet by Jenny and became the new vicar of St Michael and All Angels just before Christmas. Don't you see? So

6

many wonderful things have happened, and in such a small village.'

'Yes, I know. But why is all that such a problem?'

'I'm simply saying that it's almost too good to be true. All those people were strangers, give or take a few, but the minute they set foot in Little Pondale, everything fell into place. Everyone got what they wanted and much, much more besides. And in a relatively short period of time.'

'Oh I see.' Jet smiled and coaxed a wayward strand of her hair back into her bun. 'You're adopting Hettie's philosophy, are you? When life is running smoothly, watch out for a bump in the road.' His chest rose and fell as he chuckled and she lifted her head to look him straight in the eye.

'No. Not really. But she does have a point. Life isn't usually like this, is it? I mean, it's not normally so fabulous for everyone. It's as if Little Pondale is a jigsaw puzzle and all the bits have slotted perfectly into place. That never happens. There's always one bit missing. A bit it usually takes ages to find. But not here. Take Cathy and Christy, for example. Two best friends who are single mums rent Corner Cottage from me so that their young daughters, Daisy and Dylan can have the perfect Christmas. They're only supposed to be here for two weeks, but what happens? Cathy falls in love with fellow holiday maker, Leo, and Christy falls for Toby when she helps out in The Frog and Lily over an exceptionally busy

Christmas and New Year. We even get masses of snow, so the village looks more beautiful and is the perfect setting for romance. And now Cathy, Christy, Daisy and Dylan are living in Corner Cottage for the foreseeable future, and Leo's joined Cathy there and insists on paying rent, even though I told him I don't need the money and it somehow feels wrong because they've become our friends.'

Jet laughed. 'You'll never be a ruthless business woman, will you? It's just as well Mattie left you so much money. Not that I'm complaining. I love the fact that you want to share your good fortune with everyone. And I agree. A lot of good things have happened here in a seemingly short time frame, but that's simply because Little Pondale *is* such a wonderful place.'

Jet was right on both counts. Mia would never make any money from the property she now owned, which was fine with her. She had refused to charge Ella and Gill rent for Sunbeam Cottage even though they had the place to themselves since she had moved in with Jet. But Leo Hardman had insisted on paying the market rent for Corner Cottage, no matter what Mia said. Even Cathy and Christy offered to pay their share but Leo wouldn't hear of that. Which was probably just as well. Neither Cathy nor Christy were well-off, although Cathy had told Mia that her grandad had left her a small inheritance. Being a banker, Leo could afford it, despite the fact he lived and worked in

London during the week and only came back to Little Pondale on Friday evenings. Mia would have happily let them all stay there for free, but he was adamant that rent should be paid, so eventually, Mia had reluctantly agreed. But she had told Jet right away that she would put the money aside to go towards something special for the village next Christmas – after paying tax, of course, and she would tell everyone that Leo had paid for it. And Jet was also right about Little Pondale being a wonderful place. Mia couldn't imagine herself living anywhere else now.

'And I love the fact you agree to me spending the money on things like reindeer, even though it means more work on the farm.' She kissed him on his cheek.

'It's your money, Mia. You can spend it on anything you want.' He kissed the tip of her nose. 'Are you over your nightmare now? Can we go back to sleep?'

Mia grinned. 'It's *our* money, Jet. How many times do I have to say that? And we could go back to sleep. If you really want to. Or we could do something else.'

Jet returned her grin. 'Have I told you lately how much I love you, Mia Ward?' He gently rolled her onto her back.

'Not since yesterday,' she said, giggling like a naughty schoolgirl as she wrapped her arms around him, her body already tingling from his touch.

But afterwards, when she fell asleep, she had the dream again and woke up, sobbing loudly.

Jet was awake within seconds. 'Another bad dream?' He pulled her back into his arms.

She nodded wearily. 'The same one, I think. Even though I can't remember it. Oh God, Jet. Something dreadful is going to happen. I'm sure it is.'

He comforted her again. 'It isn't, Mia. Trust me. We all have bad dreams once in a while, but they don't very often come true. You'll see. Everything will be fine in the morning and you'll wonder why you were so upset by it. I know it's easy for me to say, but I don't think you should be worrying about things going too well. Let's simply enjoy it while it is. There's enough doom and gloom in the world what with Brexit and everything else. We shouldn't be looking for more. Besides, I know you said you're worried that things are going far too well for everyone but last year wasn't all perfect, was it? Or have you already forgotten about Tom and Alexia?'

Mia shook her head. 'Of course not.' Jet had a point. Yes, everything was wonderful now but last year had a few downs and one or two unpleasant surprises. Perhaps those were the bad times and these were the good. She needed to remind herself of that, not dwell on a bad dream. 'You're right. I should be enjoying the sunshine, not looking for clouds.' That was another of Hettie's snippets of wisdom. The woman had such a gem for every conceivable eventuality and it seemed that Mia had filed them in her brain. 'But I can't shake the feeling that we're going to get some awful news or something. I know it was only a dream, but …' She let her voice trail off. She shouldn't let a dream spoil reality. Just because everything was going brilliantly for all of them, it didn't mean that would change. That something would suddenly go wrong. Did it? Yes, Hettie would say that one had to expect the bad along with the good, but if life was good, should a person actually look for the bad? Was that what she was doing? And if she really thought about it, there were one or two things that weren't quite so good.

When Freda and Alec Bywater had returned from their Spanish holiday just a few days ago and announced they were planning to retire to Spain, that was both good and bad news, wasn't it? It was met with a mixture of joy and sadness, not merely by Toby, who was ecstatic at the prospect of taking over The Frog and Lily from his parents, but also by everyone else in the village. On the one hand, they were thrilled for all concerned. On the other, Toby wouldn't be the only one to miss Freda and Alec. Toby had brightened noticeably when Mia suggested that Christy might be willing to move into the pub and help out on a permanent basis and that plan would suit all involved, not only Toby and Christy. It would also give Cathy and Leo the privacy and space to deepen their relationship. Mia had seen the good in what was also bad news, in a way, so why couldn't she do the same with this dream? If something bad was going to happen, perhaps she should try to look for something good to come out of it.

And what on earth did she have to be anxious about?

She hadn't set the date for her wedding yet. Perhaps that was what was niggling at her. Or perhaps she was getting pre-wedding jitters? No. That was ridiculous. She didn't have any qualms about marrying Jet. He was the love of her life. She was certain of that beyond a shadow of a doubt.

Perhaps Jet was right about her dreams. Maybe it was the blue cheese, after all.

'Well, it's five in the morning,' Jet said, a hint of amusement in his voice despite it being the third time they were both awake. 'I've got to be up in an hour. It seems that every time you go back to sleep, you have the same bad dream. We may as well do something to take your mind off it, and to keep ourselves occupied until it's time for me to get up.' He wrapped his arms more tightly around her and shifted his agile body into the perfect position.

Mia grinned. 'Do a jigsaw puzzle, do you mean? We tried sex earlier and it didn't work.'

Jet grinned back. 'We need to try harder. Last time we only spent fifteen minutes or so. This time we've got an hour.' He kissed her on the lips before slowly moving his kisses downwards and

12

after a while, Mia completely forgot about the horrible dream. She forgot about everything except how wonderful it was to be Jet Cross' fiancée.

It was only when she awoke much later and Jet had gone, that the ominous feeling came flooding back. As she waited for the kettle to boil, she couldn't help but wonder whether something dreadful really was about to happen.

'Morning gorgeous.' Jet let in a cold blast of early morning, January air when he opened the door which led from the farm yard at the side of the house, into the kitchen. Little M scampered in behind him, her claws clacking on the tiles as she raced to her bed in front of the Range. 'Just got up?'

Mia struggled to open her eyes and more so to return Jet's beaming smile. 'No. I've been up for hours. It takes time for me to look this good.'

Covering the distance between them in a matter of seconds, Jet pulled her into his arms, stifling yet another of Mia's yawns by kissing her firmly on the lips.

'You always look good to me.' The twinkle in his eyes as he eased away showed he meant it.

'Ditto.' She tucked her hands beneath his padded, weatherproof jacket, wrapped her arms around his solid waist and kissed him back but as he loosened the belt of her dressing gown and slid one hand inside her pyjama top, she shrieked. 'God, Jet! Your hand's freezing.'

He grinned at her. 'It's cold outside. I need warming up.'

Mia gently pushed him away but she grinned back. 'Then go and sit in front of the Range. Besides, I'm far too exhausted right now. I'm having enough trouble standing up, let alone doing anything else.'

'You don't have to stand.' He nodded his head towards the large kitchen table and winked.

Mia raised her brows. 'In your dreams.' Although it wouldn't be the first time the kitchen table had seen that sort of action since Mia and Jet started dating. And possibly some of the girls he'd previously dated had been treated to his abundant charms on the pine surface – but Mia told herself she wouldn't ever think about his former conquests. She couldn't really call them girlfriends because he hadn't stayed with any of them long enough to have a relationship. If the village gossip she had heard when she first arrived was true, there were too many to count. She simply revelled in the knowledge that from now on, she would be the only one. 'Franklin and Pete are outside. As much as I love you, I'd rather they didn't pop their heads around the kitchen door and find us sprawled across the table.'

Jet threw her one of his devilish grins. 'Did you manage to get any sleep after I brought you coffee earlier?' He slipped off his jacket, hung it on the back of a chair and walked to the worktop, taking a couple of mugs from the wall cupboard.

Mia shook her head and yawned. 'Hardly any, but when I turned over to drink the coffee it was cold so I must've nodded off, I suppose.'

He smiled. 'Sit down sleepyhead. I'll make a fresh pot.'

'The kettle's almost boiled.' It flicked off as she spoke.

'I want proper coffee. Not instant.' He smiled again as he set about making the coffee and grabbed a loaf of bread, cutting several thick slices. 'Want some toast?'

Mia nodded. 'Yes please.' She flopped onto a chair and yawned for the umpteenth time. 'I'll get dressed in a minute and go and feed the reindeer.'

That was her favourite job on Jet's farm and since getting the reindeer shortly before Christmas, one she had taken to with surprising gusto. Jet often joked that only a few months ago she didn't know one end of a cow from the other and now she was taking to farm work like a duck to water.

That wasn't quite true. She still didn't like feeding the chickens. There were too many of them and each time she opened the barn door, or saw them rummaging around outside she envisaged a scene from that famous film, *The Birds*. The fact that these chickens were free range only made it worse. That meant they could go anywhere they liked. A few of them even trotted into the kitchen from time to time. And as for milking the cows. Forget it. She tried it once, got sprayed in the face with thick, warm milk, and announced then and there she wouldn't be doing that again. She was willing to help out making cheese in the Little Pond Farm cheese factory. Not a factory in its real sense, just one of the small sheds in the farm yard, but she needed to learn the ropes and somehow she hadn't got around to finding the time for Jet to show her.

'No need.' Jet glanced over his shoulder. 'Franklin fed them first thing. I told him you might be having a lie-in because you didn't get much sleep. I think they miss the snow now that's it's all melted but there was a hard frost last night and the ground is completely white this morning so they're in their element in the field. The chickens have been fed, the cows milked and we've started making the first batch of cheese. We're well ahead of schedule so you can spend the day lounging in bed or on the sofa if you like.'

'There must be something you need a hand with.' Another yawn escaped her. It turned into a grin when he smiled mischievously and raised his brows several times in rapid succession. 'I'm being serious.'

'So am I.' He winked at her before turning away to deal with the toast. 'Honestly, we're fine. You get some sleep. You looked shattered.'

'You said I looked good.' Her tone held a note of mock indignation.

'You do. But you also look shattered. I'll light the fire in the sitting room and after breakfast I think you should have a shower, get dressed and

16

then take a nap on the sofa. Franklin said Lori's going to pop round later for coffee. You don't want your mum to start worrying about you, so get some rest before she sees you. That's an order.' He placed a plate of toast, the butter dish and a jar of marmalade in front of her and tried to look assertive.

'Yes, oh lord and master. As always I'll obey your every command.'

He raised his brows. 'I wish.' He pulled a face as the kitchen landline phone rang. Obviously recognising the number on the caller display, he smiled. 'Hi Bear. How's things?'

Mia watched the colour drain from his handsome face, the grey pallor contrasting sharply with the black sheen of his hair. Concern, then shock replaced the twinkle in his eyes and when he looked across at her, the lines etched around them and the tightness of his mouth made it abundantly clear that Rupert, otherwise known as Bear, had given Jet bad news.

And not simply bad news. Something dreadful had happened if the expression on Jet's face was anything to go by.

Chapter Two

'What's happened?' Mia sat bolt upright.

'I'll be right there,' Jet said into the phone before meeting Mia's eyes and hanging up. The lines on his face had softened and he let out a small sigh of relief. 'It's Alec. He's had a heart attack. But he's alive.'

'Oh my God!' Mia jumped to her feet and hurried to Jet's side. Now was not the time to say, 'I told you so.' But Jet said it for her.

'It seems you were right about something bad happening.' He sounded as shocked as she was as she slid her arms around his waist. 'Bear says Alec may need surgery, but he's managed to stabilise him and they're waiting for an ambulance. Bear's got to perform a couple of ops himself, on a dog and a cat, so he's asked if I could take Freda and Toby to the hospital. Neither of them is fit to drive in the state of shock they're in and they can't both go in the ambulance.'

'Well, that's some good news.' Mia looked up into Jet's eyes. 'That Alec's alive, I mean. Shall I come with you?'

Jet shook his head. 'I'm leaving right now. Bear's got to get back to his surgery the minute the ambulance arrives and he doesn't want to leave Freda and Toby in case they decide they're okay to drive. I'll call you as soon as I hear anything.' He gave her a quick kiss on the lips, grabbed his jacket and dashed towards the hall leading to the front door of the farmhouse. Little M instantly scrambled out of her bed to follow.

'Stay, Little M,' Mia commanded.

The dog glanced from the hall to Mia before lowering her head and reluctantly trotting back to her bed where she picked up one of the toys she received at Christmas and snuggled down with it beside her.

Moments later, Mia heard the front door bang shut, Jet's car door slam, and the roar of the engine, followed by the screech of tyres as he sped down the drive towards the village.

Mia poured herself a second cup of coffee and returned to her seat, her mind racing and her heart pounding. Had this been the awful thing she had dreamt about? But how could she have known Alec would have a heart attack? Well, strictly speaking, she hadn't. She had merely had a dreadful feeling that something bad was going to happen – and it had. Nevertheless, it seemed her intuition was spot on.

Thankfully, it wasn't as bad as it could have been – although having a heart attack was serious enough; there was no denying that. But Alec had survived. Bear might not be a doctor but he was a 'first responder' and as a vet, too, he knew what he was doing. Alec was in good hands until the ambulance got to him. Surgery could be dangerous but Alec was strong and would pull through. Wouldn't he?

Poor Freda though. She and Alec were devoted to one another. She would be going through hell. And so would Toby. He idealised his dad.

Did Alexia know? Would anyone have phoned her in Spain to tell her? How would she take the news? Especially after the horrid things she had said to her parents last year before she went to prison. But they had patched things up in Spain. Toby had told Mia at the New Year's Eve party in the pub that his mum and dad were having a wonderful holiday and that Alexia had 'calmed down and regretted everything', according to his dad. Someone would call her. Of course they would.

Mia almost felt sorry for Alexia. She remembered how devastated she had been when her own dad had died. She wouldn't wish that on anyone. Not even her worst enemy. Not even Alexia.

But Alec wasn't dead. Mia must banish all negative thoughts. Alec would have an op and he would be fine and Alexia wouldn't need to worry. Except she might. Being far away at such a time would make anyone concerned.

Mia jumped when the landline rang again.

It was too soon to be an update from Jet. Was it Bear calling back to give more bad news? Had Alec taken a turn for the worse?

Somewhat reluctantly, Mia got up to answer it and was relieved to see Ella's name appear on the caller display. She'd probably heard about Alec. No doubt from Hettie who had a knack of being the first to know anything that happened in the village ... most of the time.

'Hi, Ella. If you're calling to tell me the awful news, I already know. Bear called a few minutes ago and Jet's dashed to the pub to be with Freda and Toby.'

'W-what? How?' Ella sobbed down the line. 'Wait. F-Freda and Toby? What?'

'Ella! Are you crying? Why are you crying? It's sad I know, but it's not as if we're that close to Alec really. And he's alive and ...' Mia hesitated. 'Ella?' Her fingers tightened around the handset, a knot the size of an acorn formed in her stomach. 'Ella? Are you upset about Alec? Or has something else happened? Are you okay? Is it ... is it Gill? Has something happened to Gill?'

Ella tried to speak between sobs but Mia couldn't understand her garbled words. Apart from one.

Garrick.

The knot in Mia's stomach moved towards her heart.

'Ella? Has … has something happened to Garrick? Or the baby? God, Ella! Tell me. What is it?'

Ella gasped, sobbed, sucked in a loud breath and finally managed: 'It's … n-not Garrick. Or Flora. It's … it's Fiona. She's dead, Mia. Fi-Fiona's dead!'

'Dead? Fiona?' It took a few seconds for the terrible news to sink in after the overwhelming relief that it wasn't Garrick. 'How? When? Are you sure?'

'Of c-course I am! Garrick … called a few minutes ago.'

'Stay there. I'm coming round.'

Without waiting for a reply, Mia hung up, raced to the hall, grabbed her coat, shoved on her boots and dashed to her car. It was only when she tried to put the coat on as she ran and couldn't understand why it was such a struggle, that she realised she wasn't dressed. Did it matter? It might if Ella needed her to go out and get something. Mia hesitated for a second, raced back inside, kicked off her boats, tossed the coat on the hall table, and took the stairs two at a time. Less than five minutes later, she jumped down several stairs at once, grabbed her coat again, slid her bare feet in her boots and dashed to the car. Now all that mattered was getting to Ella.

As she sped down the drive, she remembered about Little M. But she couldn't take the dog with her. She'd have to call her mum and ask her to nip up to the farm to tell Franklin. Bugger! Why wasn't there any mobile phone reception in this damn village? Most of the time it was a slight inconvenience not being able to make a call or send a text unless you went to the top of Frog Hill, or climbed the three hundred steps in the steeple of St Michael and All Angels, but at times like this. Well. It was nothing short of a disaster.

There was no point in fretting over it now. She'd call her mum from the landline at Sunbeam Cottage and Lori would drive the short distance to the farmyard, or maybe even walk the mile or so, and let Franklin know. He'd make sure Little M was all right. The dog didn't mind being left alone for an hour or two but Mia had no idea how long she would be. Or when Jet might be back. Perhaps she should ask her mum to look after Little M until she had a better idea of what was happening.

God, what a mess. Mia had expected something bad to happen – but two things? Two terrible things such as these. One after the other. No way.

At least Alec was alive. Could it be true about Fiona? Was she really dead? It wasn't possible, was it? Only two weeks ago, Fiona had given birth to a baby girl. Garrick's baby. Both mother and baby were fine. Mia had seen photos of baby Flora in Fiona's arms – with proud dad, Garrick by

Fiona's side, smiling adoringly at his daughter. Ella and Gill had gone to Scotland to see them and Fiona was fit and well two days ago when they had returned. How could she now be dead? Ella must've got it wrong. She must have. Perhaps there'd been an accident and Fiona was in intensive care or something. But dead? Fiona couldn't possibly be dead. She was only just thirty-three. A few months younger than Mia.

But as Mia tore down the lane from the farm and burst onto Seaside Road, only half-looking to see if the road was clear, something inside her told her it was true. Fiona, the woman Garrick had left Mia for, to spend his life with, was dead. That meant Garrick was a single dad with a baby girl only two weeks old.

How could life be so cruel? How could it play such dreadful tricks on people? How could it make everyone believe that life was good and everything was as it should be – and then do this? It wasn't fair. It wasn't right. Poor Fiona. Poor baby Flora. Poor, dear Garrick. He must be devastated. How would he cope with this? He'd need his sister. And his family.

He'd also need a good friend. And Mia would do anything she could to help him.

Anything at all.

Chapter Three

When Mia arrived at Sunbeam Cottage, she and
Ella spent at least five minutes in tears, hugging
one another and trying to make sense out of
something that made no sense at all.

'Did Garrick say what happened?' Mia asked,
as soon as she was able, still hugging her friend so
tight that Ella made a joke that if Mia didn't let her
go, she'd be dead too. It was in appalling taste,
they both knew that, but nothing seemed to matter
anymore.

They walked towards the kitchen, Ella much
calmer now that Mia was by her side.

'To be honest, both of us were in complete
shock. Garrick, because he was still at the hospital
and couldn't believe Fiona was really dead. Me,
because it felt like I'd been hit by a bus and
couldn't get up. All I kept saying, I think, was
something along the lines of, 'How can she be
dead? She's just had a baby, and she's far too

young to die.' Ella shook her head in self-censure as if she felt she had failed miserably in consoling her twin brother.

Gill, who was in the kitchen making coffee, nodded. 'I tried to speak to Garrick to get some answers, but the guy was devastated. Completely out of it. He kept repeating, "She's dead. Fiona's dead." Even when I asked him how, he simply said the same thing over and over again. Then he said he'd call back later and suddenly hung up. So we have no idea what happened or how she died.'

'Or what to do next,' Ella added, collapsing onto a chair at the kitchen table as if all her energy had been sucked out of her. 'I wanted to get the first flight to Scotland to be with him, but I don't know where he is. I can't call him back. He didn't give us the number. Or the name of the hospital. Or say where he would be. What if he comes here and I'm up there?'

'He won't come here,' Gill said, placing a mug of coffee in front of Ella and waiting for Mia to sit down before handing her a mug. 'He's got a baby to look after, details to sort out and a funeral to arrange. He'll need to stay put for a while at least, I should think.' He glanced at Mia. 'The number on the caller display came up as withheld as they always do with large organisations and such, so we don't know which hospital it is. I was going to do a search for hospitals near to where they live and then give each one a call until one of them recognised either Garrick or Fiona's names, but Ella wants to keep the line free in case Garrick calls back.'

'Oh. I wanted to give Mum a quick call. I've left Little M at home and Jet's taken Toby and Freda to the hospital to be with Alec.'

'Alec?' Ella gave Mia an odd look.

'Why?' Gill asked, simultaneously. 'Has something happened to Alec?'

Mia's hand shot to her mouth. 'Oh my God! I didn't tell you, did I? I thought that was why you'd called me but … sorry.' She shook her head to clear her mind. 'Alec's had a heart attack. He's okay, but Bear says he may need surgery. Jet left to be with Freda and Toby just a few minutes before you called.'

'Jesus!' Gill said.

Ella didn't say anything at first and from the expression on her face it seemed as if she was having trouble taking it in, but after a moment or two she said: 'Call Lori. But try to be quick in case Garrick calls back.'

It only took Mia a few seconds to tell her mum the terrible news and Lori told her not to worry. She'd deal with it.

Twenty minutes or so later, Lori arrived at Sunbeam Cottage.

'Franklin's looking after Little M,' she said, giving Mia a hearty hug as soon as she walked in. 'And when Jet gets back, or calls, he'll tell him where you are.' She turned to Ella and gave her an even bigger hug. 'I'm so, so sorry, sweetheart. Have you taken anything for the shock?'

'Brandy,' Gill said, standing behind them.

'I could do with another,' Ella said.

'I wouldn't mind one,' added Mia. 'I still can't believe all this.'

'I'll get them.' Gill walked towards the sitting room and the cocktail cabinet. 'Would you like one, Lori, or would you rather something else?' he called over his shoulder.

'Not for me, thanks.' She took Ella's hands in hers. 'Garrick will need you, Ella. Or your mum and dad. Or probably all of you. Have you spoken to them?'

'Mum and Dad?' The surprise on Ella's face was evident. It was as if she had completely forgotten her parents. 'No, I …' She shrugged, darted a look at Mia and then gave Lori a pitiful look. 'I didn't want the phone to be engaged in case Garrick calls back.'

'I think you should call them,' Lori said.

But one second later the phone rang and it was them phoning Ella.

After more tears and a fairly lengthy conversation, Ella hung up.

'Dad managed to get more out of Garrick than I did. At least he knows where Garrick is. Dad's off to the airport now and should be there by midday, so Garrick won't be alone for too long, and he's got Flora with him, so Dad said, so at least we know she's okay. Dad could only get one seat this morning but he's booked seats for me and Mum on the early evening flight. They assumed I'd want to be there, and Mum and I can go together.'

'That makes perfect sense,' Gill said, handing Ella the glass of brandy he had poured while she was on the phone. 'I'll drive you up to London whenever you're ready to go.'

'I can get the train if you'll drop me at the station. It's not fair to ask you to drive to London and back again all in one afternoon. But I think I need this drink first. And to sit down for another five minutes. My legs feel like jelly and my head like it's about to fall off.'

Gill shook his head. 'I'll take you to London. And I'll also take you and your mum to the airport. Don't argue, Ella. You're not going by train and you're not taking a cab to Gatwick.'

Ella flopped down on her chair. 'But it'll take you hours to drive all that way. You'll be shattered.'

'It's just over an hour to your mum's. We'll stop for a cup of tea, then it's fifty minutes or so to Gatwick. I'll grab a coffee while you're waiting to depart, and I'll be home again in time for supper, by which time you'll be calling to tell me you've arrived safely in Aberdeen.'

'You can come to us for supper if you like, Gill,' Mia offered. 'Ella can call you there and that way I'll know she's safe too, without making her call us both.' She gave Ella a sympathetic smile.

29

'Sounds good to me,' Gill said. 'Thanks.'

'Okay,' said Ella.

The doorbell rang and Gill went to see who was there.

'It might be Jet,' Mia said.

'Too soon, I think,' said Lori.

Gill must have been reluctant to let the person in because he was gone for several seconds until Ella called out: 'Whoever it is, for God's sake let them in, Gill. Or tell them to sod off. I don't care which. Just shut the bloody door because it's letting the freezing cold in.'

'Coo-ey,' Hettie's voice rang out. 'It's only me, deary.'

Knowing Hettie, she had probably taken her chance and barged past Gill because if he had had his way at a time like this, he'd probably have preferred to tell her to go away – a slightly more polite version of Ella's sentiments.

Hettie shuffled down the hall and across the kitchen to Ella and hugged her tight.

'You poor dear thing. My heart is breaking at your news, deary.'

'How did you hear the news?' Gill asked, looking confused. 'You didn't say.'

Hettie glanced around the room. 'From Billy, the postman. He was delivering a parcel to the farmhouse and needed a signature from Mia. That's when Franklin told him.' She smiled at Mia. 'Don't worry, deary. Billy let Franklin sign for it.'

Mia frowned. 'I'm not worried about a bloody parcel, Hettie. That's the last thing on my mind.'

'I'm sorry, Ella,' Lori said, sighing. 'I should've told Franklin not to say anything.'

'Why?' Ella sounded annoyed. 'Everyone's going to know sooner or later. Although I'd rather they didn't all come to pay their respects or whatever.' She glared at Hettie.

'Would you rather I hadn't come, deary? I'll go if you want.' Hettie crossed her arms beneath her ample bosom and pouted. 'I was worried about you, that's all, and wanted to make sure you were all right.'

'All right? I don't know if I'm coming or going, Hettie.' Ella ran a hand through her tousled blonde hair and sighed. 'But I shouldn't take that out on you. Sorry. Sit down and have a cup of tea.'

Mia was worried. She'd never seen Ella like this. One minute she was in floods of tears, the next, behaving almost as if nothing had happened. But perhaps that's what a shock like this does to you. Mia wasn't feeling quite herself either.

'No need to apologise to me, deary. You've just lost your sister-in-law so you're entitled to be upset.' Hettie pulled out a chair and sat. 'Although they hadn't actually got around to getting married yet, had they, deary? So the poor dear wasn't related by law. It doesn't make it any easier though, I realise that. Oh. Shall I make the tea?' She glanced around at everyone.

Lori tutted and placed a hand on Gill's shoulder. He'd just sat down and was about to get up again. 'No, Hettie. I'll do it. Why don't you take a few deep breaths? You must be exhausted from telling anyone you could, the awful news.'

Hettie didn't even try to deny that veiled accusation. 'And not just this news, my dears. There's also poor, dear Alec. Although he's alive of course, so that's not quite as dreadful.'

'I sometimes wonder how you've managed to live to such a ripe old age, Hettie,' Gill said, his words dripping with sarcasm as he reached out and wrapped an arm around Ella as if to shield her from Hettie. Not that Ella appeared to have taken in what was being said. Once again she had a faraway look in her eyes and an expression on her face as if she were deep in thought.

'It's having someone to love, deary,' Hettie said, oblivious to the sarcasm. 'That's the trick to a long life. After I lost my darling Hector, I thought it wouldn't be long until I joined him in his grave. Not that he was buried, but you know what I mean. But then our darling Matilda moved into this very cottage, and her friendship gave me a new lease of life. And she gave me Prince Gustav, of course. And you all know how much I adore that little rat of mine. And now I have Fred. So I think I've a good few years more ahead of me, my dears.'

'Oh joy,' Ella said, but she didn't look at all pleased by the prospect. Perhaps she had been listening to the conversation, after all.

'Everyone in the village is devastated by the news,' Hettie continued, clearly unwilling to let the subject drop and probably trying to glean more information. It also confirmed the suspicion that she'd told as many people as possible. You could always count on Hettie to do that. 'First Alec's heart attack then that poor, dear girl dying. Just like that. None of us can take it in. And bad things always come in threes, my dears.'

Gill scowled as Lori handed Hettie a cup of tea. 'I don't think we need to hear that, Hettie, thanks all the same.' He squeezed Ella tighter but she appeared to be miles away again.

For once, Hettie seemed nonplussed. 'What, deary? Oh. You're probably right. I wasn't thinking. Sorry. You know me. Talking ten chickens at a time.' She stared into the cup and didn't utter another word.

But nor did anyone else. Mia sipped her second brandy as everyone glanced at one another from time to time as if they thought they should be saying something; they simply had no idea what. Mia was heartbroken for her friend, but on occasions such as this, sometimes silence was as comforting as words. Sometimes even more so.

Chapter Four

'Life's unpredictable,' Lori said, as she and Mia walked across the village green towards Lake's Bakes, two days later. 'Everyone knows that. And there's only one thing certain about it – we're all going to shuffle off this mortal coil at some point, whether we're ready to or not.'

'I get that,' said Mia, her boots scrunching on the frost-covered grass. She was still struggling to come to terms with the events of the last few days. Despite her bad dreams, she hadn't expected anything quite like this. Alec's heart attack was awful enough, but his operation had gone smoothly and now, only two days later, he was able to sit up in his hospital bed, so that was one tragedy averted. On the other hand, Fiona dying so suddenly and at such a young age, was simply too dreadful to comprehend. 'What I don't get is why it had to be Fiona. And why now? Two weeks after having a baby? It's just so wrong. So unfair. So cruel. And for me to have had those dreams the night before we got the news, is really freaky. Hettie says I may have psychic leanings but I haven't learnt how to tap into them.'

Lori raised her brows and tutted, tugging her coat tighter and adjusting her scarf. 'Hettie says a lot of things, as we all know, and most of them should be taken with a pinch of salt. If you had psychic leanings you would've known about them long before now, sweetheart.'

'Then how do you explain the dreams?'

Lori shrugged. 'I can't. But as you can't remember what they were about, we'll never know whether they had anything to do with what happened. Personally, I think you're like your dear father. He was one of those people who worried if everything was going too well.'

'Yes. Well. As he also died young, he may've had good cause to worry.' Mia's gloved hand shot to her mouth. She was horrified she'd said that. 'Oh God, I'm so sorry, Mum. I didn't mean that.' Losing her dad had been devastating and she still missed him every day. So did her mum, despite Lori having recently been given a second chance at love.

'That's all right, darling. We both loved Ernest dearly and it was a long time ago. But worrying is stressful, and stress is one of the biggest causes of heart attacks. I read that somewhere. So you should try not to worry about what the future may hold, and learn to take each day as it comes.'

'To live each day as if it's our last, you mean. That's what Jet said when he found out about Fiona. Once he'd got over the shock, that is. He couldn't believe it either. No one can. And this sounds awful, but I keep having to remind myself she's gone. It's so unreal.'

'I think that's how everyone feels when someone passes away so suddenly. It takes time to sink in. To accept the reality of the situation. And Jet's right. We should treat each day as if it may be our last. And we should be kind to people. Tell those we love that we love them. Not put off doing the things we want to do, because by postponing them, we may never get the chance to do them. That's why Franklin doesn't believe in 'bucket lists'. Instead of making a list of all the exciting adventures we want to have in the future, he says we should simply get off our butts and go and have them. Because by tomorrow, it may be too late.'

'That's a cheery thought.' Mia pushed open the door of the bakery and along with a blast of warm air, the comforting aroma of freshly baked bread, together with hints of vanilla, cinnamon and other spices wafted towards her as the little bell above the door, tinkled overhead. 'Actually, there's another certainty in life. It's full of surprises. And they're not always good. Unlike the heavenly fragrance in this shop.'

'Hi Mia. Hi Lori. Have you heard from Ella?' Jenny shoved her wild red hair back into the large clip that was clearly struggling to keep it under control, and smiled sympathetically. 'I still can't believe the news. Not that I knew Fiona. Or Garrick, but it's awful, isn't it? At least Alec's doing well. That's one small mercy. But Garrick must be shell-shocked.'

Mia nodded. 'He is. And when Ella told us how Fiona died, we all were. It was bad enough before, but once you know the details, well. It's simply devastating. Obviously it's fifty times as bad for Garrick. Ella said he's walking around like a zombie. He's not sleeping, hardly eating and just keeps blaming himself. It's a good thing Ella and Mrs Swann are there to help look after baby Flora. Not that Ella's much help in that department. She's not a natural when it comes to children. Don't look at me like that, Mum. Ella said that herself last night.'

'I'm sure she's doing her best,' Lori said. 'Especially at such a difficult time.'

Jenny shook her head. 'I wouldn't know what to do or say in such a situation, even if it was my brother. I suppose you just have to be there for them, give them a hug when they need it, and show them they're not alone. They're very close, aren't they? Ella and Garrick, I mean. I know they're twins but it doesn't always follow that twins will get along. From the way she talks about him, they've got a really good relationship.'

Mia nodded. 'Incredibly so. The whole family is close. That's one good thing. Garrick will have plenty of help to get him through this.'

'Why does he blame himself?' Lori asked, frowning as if she didn't understand and had been trying to figure it out.

Mia shrugged. 'Because he thinks he should've gone to the shop instead of Fiona.'

Lori tutted. 'That's just silly. Then the lorry would've careered into him and he'd be dead instead.'

Mia pulled a face. 'I think that's the point, Mum.'

'Survivor's guilt, I believe they call that,' Jenny said, shaking her head.

'Utter nonsense, they should call it.' Lori looked cross. 'It wasn't Garrick's fault. It was black ice on the road, appalling weather, and a lorry driver who was possibly driving too fast in such conditions and didn't respond to the situation quickly enough. He's the one who should be feeling guilty, if anyone should. Not Garrick. Of course, the man may have done everything right, and still lost control. These things do happen. It could simply have been a tragic accident and no one's fault at all.'

Mia took off her gloves and slipped them in her coat pocket before loosening her scarf.

'I know. Ella said their Dad's been saying something similar. But when Fiona asked Garrick to look after Flora while she popped out to get some milk, he feels he should've insisted on going for her.' Mia glanced at Jenny to fill her in on the details she'd got from Ella. 'It was snowing heavily and was getting dark, but Fiona told him she wanted to get some fresh air because she'd been inside with Flora all day. She said she had a perfectly good pair of legs and was more than capable of walking to the corner shop, so he made a joke about her legs being better than good, and let her go without another word.'

Lori shook her head. 'I can only imagine what must've gone through his mind when he heard the crash.'

Mia nodded. 'He told Ella that although it happened three houses away, he felt their own house shake.'

'At least it was instantaneous,' said Lori, lowering her voice as if out of respect and, as Mia had done, loosening her scarf and removing her gloves. 'Fiona wouldn't have known what happened.'

'Unless she turned and saw the lorry careering towards her.' Mia shuddered. 'What an awful thought.'

The three of them fell silent for a second or two until the overhead bell tinkled and Christy came in, carrying her daughter, Dylan in her arms.

'Hello,' she said, an anxious look on her face. 'I suppose it's pointless to ask how Ella's doing? But how are you, Mia?'

Mia smiled half-heartedly. 'I'm okay thanks, and Ella's coping, I think, but obviously it's not easy.'

'Tell me about it,' said Christy. 'I can't imagine what your friend Garrick must be feeling. Toby was bad enough over his dad's episode, as everyone is calling it now. God knows what he'd have been like if Alec hadn't pulled through.'

'I hear he's sitting up in bed,' Lori said.

Christy nodded as she removed Dylan's bobble hat and ran her fingers through the child's tousled locks. Dylan raised her hands to push her mum's away while vigorously shaking her little head and saying: 'No, Mummy. No.'

Christy smiled and took off Dylan's pink, sparkly, knitted mittens. 'Yeah. Toby says Alec's hoping to come home in a few days. Freda's got other ideas of course, and doesn't want him home until the doctors are absolutely certain there's no chance of him having another episode.'

'They won't be moving to Spain anytime soon, I'm guessing,' Jenny said, leaning on the counter and smiling at Dylan.

'Nope. Those plans have been temporarily put on hold. But Alec's adamant they're still going. Of course, that may change now Alexia's coming back and—'

'What?' Mia's mouth fell open and she darted a look at her mum, who appeared equally surprised. Mia stared at Christy. 'Did you just say Alexia's coming back? To Little Pondale?'

'Yep. Oh, I see.' Christy's expression showed she understood. 'That's probably not something you wanted to hear, given what went on. Toby's not best pleased himself, between you and me. He hasn't seen his sister since the day she went to prison. He loves her, naturally, and Freda and Alec assure us Alexia is a changed woman. But, well, you know.'

'Mummy?' Dylan wriggled in Christy's arms and tapped her on the face. 'Look at the pretty cakes. I'd like a pretty cake.'

Christy grinned. 'I bet you would.' She lowered Dylan to the ground. 'Okay then young lady. Pick a cake for you and one for Daisy. Mummy's got her eye on one of those rum babas and I know Cathy wants a sticky bun. Oh, but you were first, Mia. Wait a minute, baby.' She reached for Dylan's hand but the child twisted her body to avoid being caught and dashed to the counter where she rested her head against the glass to look at all the cakes on display, her tiny mouth forming a perfect 'O'.

Mia laughed. 'We're in no rush. I only came in for bread. You go first.'

Lori stepped aside too. 'And I just came for the walk. Although you're right, Dylan. They are very pretty cakes.' She smiled at Dylan, who was too busy drooling to notice, then glanced at Mia. 'Maybe we should get one or two for later. What do you think, sweetheart?'

'Absolutely. But you can still go first, Christy. It'll take Mum at least ten minutes to decide what she wants and twice as long to choose one for Franklin.'

Jenny grinned but as she looked over the counter towards the door, she shook her head. Still grinning she said: 'Hettie's on her way across the green. She's just passed the pond so she'll be here any second.'

All eyes turned towards the door and a moment later, Hettie burst in, puffing and panting, her chubby cheeks crimson, her eyes watering from the cold. She wiped them with a hanky she pulled from her coat pocket before beaming at everyone in the now somewhat crowded shop.

'Well, hello my dears. And hello, little angel. How are you?' She smiled tenderly at Dylan.

'Dylan, Hettie's talking to you. Say hello.'

Christy gave her daughter a gentle tap on the head with the bobble of the hat she was holding and Dylan spun round, a huge frown creasing her little brows, her hands clamped awkwardly on her hips. She sighed as if the troubles of the world were on her tiny shoulders.

'Hello,' she said, to no one in particular, and turned her attention back to the cakes.

Christy shrugged. 'Choosing a cake is a serious business. Sorry, Hettie.'

'No need, deary. I understand. I feel the same. Any more news from Ella?' Hettie placed one hand on Mia's arm.

'Not since yesterday, no.'

'Have they set a date for the funeral? Are you going? Fred and I are wondering if we should send flowers. I'm fond of Garrick, as you know and I feel we should show our respect.'

'I'm afraid I can't help you on that score. I'd like to go, but then again … I really don't like funerals. I do want to be there for Garrick though.' Mia shrugged. 'I'll let you know when I hear something.'

'Thank you, deary.'

'I have some news, Hettie,' Christy said, grinning. 'Alexia Bywater's coming back.'

Hettie's eyes grew as wide as saucers as she looked from Christy to Mia and Lori and back to Christy. 'Alexia? Coming back to Little Pondale? Well, well.' She tapped Mia's arm with her hand. 'You see, my dear. First poor Alec's episode, then sweet Fiona's passing, and now Alexia's returning to the village. I told you, didn't I, deary? Bad things always come in threes.'

Chapter Five

Jet grinned when Mia told him the news, which wasn't at all the reaction she'd expected. He burst out laughing when she told him what Hettie had said.

'So Alexia's coming home. I can't say I'm surprised. In spite of the things she said the day she was arrested, I've known her all my life and she adores Freda and Alec. Toby too, however much she might protest otherwise.'

'Doesn't it bother you?' Mia frowned as she pulled her coat tighter and shoved her gloved hands in her pockets. It was freezing earlier but if anything it had turned colder since she and Lori had left the bakery and the part of the farmyard where she and Jet were standing was open to the bitter north-east wind that had been blowing on and off all morning.

He lifted a bale of hay as if it were a duckdown pillow and tossed it onto the stack already on the back of the trailer attached to his battered Land Rover.

'Why should it bother me? Alexia wasn't the one who tried to kill me. That was Tom. And I don't think he'll be coming back here anytime soon. Once he gets out, that is.'

'But she did threaten me. And she said some pretty nasty stuff.'

'But she didn't really do anything, did she? The only reason she went to prison was because she assaulted a police officer and resisted arrest.' He stopped working and looked Mia in the eye. 'I can see why you might be apprehensive, but I honestly think that whole business was just a huge mistake on her part and that she regrets it. That's what Toby told us over New Year, remember? You even said that's what Christy told you today. That she's a changed woman. Love does funny things to us all, Mia. I can vouch for that.'

Mia gave a little gasp. 'What does that mean?'

He grinned at her. 'Don't get annoyed. All I'm saying is that when we fall madly in love with someone, it can make us do things we wouldn't normally do. It can change us in ways we could never have imagined. I changed, didn't I? Unfortunately, Alexia changed for the worse, not the better. But I think it was a temporary hiccup. Being away from Tom's influence, the brief stint in one of Her Majesty's finest lock-ups, and the respite in Spain have possibly brought her back to her senses and she's the old Alexia we all know and love.'

'Love? Really? Is that a word you want to use about one of your exes in front of your fiancée?'

Jet laughed, brushed a few large bits of hay from the front of his jacket and pulled Mia into his arms. 'I mean in a completely platonic way. You know I do. But if I'm totally honest, then yes, I suppose I do care about her.'

Mia threw him a sarcastic look. 'According to her, you didn't care about her when you dumped her, did you? She was at pains to scream that for all to hear as she was dragged into the back of the police car.'

He grew serious. 'I was a jerk back then. We all know that. All I cared about was having fun and not getting involved.' His expression softened and a wide smile spread across his face. 'And then you came along and knocked me for six and that all changed.' He bent his head to kiss her and removing her hands from her pockets, she wrapped her arms around him.

Afterwards she said: 'If you think one kiss will make me feel less hostile towards the woman, you're sadly mistaken.'

'Then why are you smiling?'

'I'm not. My face has frozen in this position because it's so damn cold out here.'

He kissed her again. 'Want me to warm you up? It's almost lunch time. I can take a break.'

The smile she was fighting to hide grew wider. 'Yes, and that's the other thing I came to tell you. Mum and I have made some soup for lunch and there's fresh bread from Jenny's and some scrumptious cakes.' She eased herself away from him. 'Tell Franklin and Pete, would you?' She walked towards the kitchen door but tossed him a provocative smile over her shoulder. 'But we haven't finished discussing Alexia, so don't think we have.'

He laughed. 'Let's just give the girl the benefit of the doubt, shall we? We've all got some bad mixed in with the good. No one's perfect. And everyone deserves a second chance.'

'I hope you still feel the same when she drops another one of those stone angels on your head. Oh God!' Mia stopped and spun round to face him. 'Sorry. I shouldn't have said that, what with Alec and Fiona and everything. I keep forgetting. I mean … I shouldn't make jokes about death when … oh, you know what I mean.'

'Don't look so worried.' Jet shook his head and gave her a reassuring smile. 'We're all having trouble coming to terms with it and you're not the only one who keeps forgetting it's really happened. It seems callous and selfish, but life goes on, Mia and we can't walk on eggshells every minute of the day. Not even Garrick would want that.'

'I know. But it feels wrong to laugh and carry on with our lives when his is so completely broken, and Alec had such a near miss too.'

'Which is why we must treasure every moment. Go and get warm. You're shivering. I'll tell Franklin and Pete it's lunchtime.'

Mia continued towards the farmhouse. She wasn't convinced about Alexia. Admittedly, Jet and everyone else had known Alexia for years, whereas she had only known her for a few months, but even so. If the woman was really so besotted with Tom, why had she still harboured a grudge towards Jet, for dumping her? And why had she made such a point of saying she hated Mia? Alexia had made it clear that she was jealous because everyone could see that Jet was head over heels in love with Mia. She'd also said she resented the fact that Garrick had chosen Mia over her. Could Alexia's feelings have really changed so much in just a couple of months?

Despite what Jet said, Mia wasn't going to be at the top of Alexia's list of friends. Or vice versa. She would give Alexia a wide berth. The less they saw of one another, the better.

Which was a bit of a pain because that meant Mia would have to stay away from The Frog and Lily, and as it was the only pub in the village, that was inconvenient, to say the least.

Chapter Six

Mia managed to avoid Alexia for three days after her return to Little Pondale. She would have liked it to have been longer but as Alexia turned up and rang the doorbell at Little Pond Farm on the Saturday morning after her arrival, Mia had no choice but to face her. She was stunned to see the woman standing on the doorstep when she opened the front door, and even more so to see that, not only did Alexia look more beautiful, but that she was holding a large bouquet of flowers in one hand and a box bearing the Lake's Bakes logo in the other. The Spanish winter sun had given Alexia's skin a golden glow and her lustrous red hair was radiant against the heavy bank of cloud hanging low in the sky.

'Hello Mia. How are you? I'm sorry to turn up unannounced but I haven't seen you around the village and I was really hoping to get an opportunity to apologise. These are for you.'

Alexia held the flowers and box a little higher. 'A small peace offering. Any chance I could come in and have a cup of coffee?' She gave one of her beautiful smiles. 'You're welcome to throw it over me, if you like. I really am truly sorry for the things I said and did last year. The only excuse I have is temporary insanity or something.'

Having been caught off-guard, Mia tried to think of a reason not to let her in, but couldn't, and as Jet appeared from the kitchen at that precise moment, the matter was taken out her hands.

'Alexia? Hi. This is a pleasant surprise.'

Something in his voice made Mia think it was anything but a surprise to Jet. Had he suggested this? He'd told Mia that he had seen Alexia a couple of times since her return. Once while walking Little M in the village, when he'd popped into the pub for a quick drink and to say hi to Toby and see how Alec was doing, and once at rugby practice. It seemed Alexia was jumping back into village life as if nothing had happened.

'Hi, Jet. I hope you don't mind me turning up like this.'

Was that a twinkle in her eye? Or had Mia imagined it?

Jet waved his arm, inviting her in. 'Of course we don't. Come in. Mia's just made a fresh pot of coffee. I'd popped in to grab a quick one.'

Alexia laughed as she stepped into the hall. How come her laugh sounded so sexy?

'A quick one? I'm not interrupting, am I?'

Jet's laugh sounded sexy too. But he always sounded sexy.

'A quick coffee. Although…' He glanced at Mia and winked, giving Alexia a brief smile. 'Sadly I've got to get back to work. I hope you don't mind. See you this afternoon?'

Alexia nodded. 'I'll be there. Don't work too hard.'

'Where?' Mia asked, seriously unimpressed by their banter.

'Rugby practice, of course.' Jet kissed Mia quickly on the lips and grinned, before turning to walk away. Glancing back over his shoulder, he added: 'You're welcome to join us. But rolling around in a muddy field isn't really your scene, is it my love?'

It wasn't. But Mia had a sudden picture of Jet and Alexia rolling around in a muddy field, and the image was so vivid she was sorely tempted to say she would go, but Jet hadn't waited for a reply.

'I hear you've got reindeer,' Alexia said, changing the subject and giving Mia her full attention. 'Everyone in the village is saying how wonderful Christmas was. Mainly because of you. I wish I'd been here. I'd love to see them sometime, if I may.' Once again she held her gifts out towards Mia.

Mia sighed. She could hardly tell Alexia to bugger off after Jet had been so welcoming. She took the flowers and the box and nodded her head towards the kitchen.

'Follow me. Do you take milk and sugar? I can't remember.'

'Just milk.' Alexia walked by Mia's side. 'I'd like to say I'm sweet enough, but we both know I wasn't sweet last year. I can understand that it might take you some time to believe this, but I really am sorry, Mia. Sometimes it feels as though I was a completely different person for all those months. As if I'd been hypnotised or something.'

'By Tom, you mean?' So she was trying to put all the blame on Tom, was she? 'Take a seat.'

Alexia pulled out a chair and sat at the kitchen table. 'Partly. But I can't put all the blame on him. I'm a grown woman. I should be able to make my own decisions. I think the truth is, I was going through a really bad patch and Tom was there for me when I thought no one else was. But how it all spiralled so out of control, I'll never really understand.'

Mia poured two mugs of coffee and joined Alexia at the table.

'Really? When we arrived here, it seemed to us that you had a pretty good life.'

Alexia fiddled with the handle of her coffee mug. 'That's the thing though, isn't it? No one truly knows how someone else is feeling, or what's actually going on with them. People may look happy and jolly on the outside, but inside they may be crying out for help, or slowly shrivelling up and dying. That's the trouble with depression and such.

There isn't a flashing light on your head saying: 'I may look fine, but I'm not.''

Mia couldn't argue with that.

'Are you saying you were suffering from depression?'

Alexia shrugged and shook her head. 'I don't know.' She looked Mia directly in the eye. 'May I be completely honest with you?'

'Please do.' Mia was tempted to add that it would make a refreshing change. But now wasn't the time to be facetious.

Alexia took a gulp of coffee before inhaling a deep breath. 'I don't want to open up old wounds, and I know Jet has changed beyond recognition since he met you. And I'm glad. I'm truly over it now. I'm over him. I just want to be friends again, if that's possible.'

Mia tensed. 'With Jet? I think that's up to him.'

'With both of you. What I mean is, you don't have to worry about me trying to flirt with him, or doing anything inappropriate.' She looked Mia directly in the eye. 'Jet is crazy about you, and I'm happy for you both. Honestly, I am. You may not believe that after the things I said, but it's the complete and unadulterated truth. No wait. Please.' She held up her hand before Mia could respond. 'I need to say this. I want to try to make you understand.' She laid her palms flat on the table and took another deep breath. 'When Jet dumped me, I was really hurt. I cared about him far more than he realised. Far more than I realised even. After some time, I thought I was over it, but I wasn't, and every time I saw him with a different woman, it was like it took a tiny chunk out of my soul. I was getting stroppy. Crying all the time – but never in front of anyone. I still had some control. It was getting harder though. Tom was the only one who noticed anything was wrong. He was my shoulder to cry on.'

That, Mia did believe. She had been taken in herself by Tom's charms and his totally disarming manner. And she'd also cried on his shoulder. The reminder of Jet's old ways though, she could've done without.

Alexia picked up her mug and sipped her coffee before continuing: 'I'm not really sure how it happened, but before I knew it, I had fallen in love with Tom. It wasn't the same as my love for Jet though. I can't explain it, but something told me I was heading down a dangerous path. I chose to ignore it. Maybe I wanted danger. I know I wanted to feel in control again after feeling so broken and so hopeless. Tom made the future seem full of possibilities. And this may surprise you, but I have to say, he was as good as Jet in bed. Sorry. I shouldn't talk about me and Jet, but what I'm trying to say is that suddenly, I was with a man who could make me forget about Jet Cross and what I'd lost, and instead, make me see all the things I could have. Which in a way was the problem. Because it gradually became clear that

Tom wasn't the good vicar everyone thought he was, and his plans for the future meant getting things from other people. I should've walked away. But strangely, it excited me. By the time he asked me to leave you those notes, I was in so deep I couldn't have got out even if I had been thinking clearly – which I definitely wasn't. Certain types of love can be toxic. Tom's love was like that. It was a sort of poison that soaked into every fibre of my being and turned me into someone the old me wouldn't have believed was possible. Does that make any sense to you?'

Mia nodded slowly. 'Yes. It does. I do believe it's possible to completely lose ourselves in certain relationships. To be so intensely in love that we don't know who we are anymore. And when that happens, if it's with the wrong type of person, that person can exert all sorts of influence over us and make us do things we wouldn't usually even consider. Not that I'm speaking from experience, just from things I've read.'

'Perhaps that's why they call it, "being madly in love". I know I was mad for a time there.' She dropped her head in her hands and shook it to and fro, hiding her face as if in shame. 'God. I still can't believe what I did. And those evil things I said, not just to you and Jet and everyone, but to Mum and Dad, and Toby.' She raised her face and the pain in her eyes was genuine. 'And to punch a policeman!' She let out a pitiful laugh. 'Now I have a record and I'll have to live with the shame long after that's erased.'

Mia gave a little cough. 'What was prison like?'

Alexia smiled wanly. 'It was a bit like a bad hotel. A very bad hotel. One that you can't get out of and where bed bugs are the least of your worries. Your fellow 'guests' are thieves and possibly murderers, although in a way I was lucky. I was in Bronzefield which was purpose-built for women in 2004. I tried to keep myself to myself as much as possible. The worst part was lock-up at six-forty-five and knowing your room wouldn't be unlocked till eight the following day. I'll tell you this. I never intend to go back. Ever. I'm not even going to get as much as a speeding ticket in future. It did give me time to think though. To reflect on my actions. Which is what it's supposed to do so, on that score, the penal system was a complete success regarding me. I honestly thought I'd get a suspended sentence, but to actually get a jail term, albeit very short, was a complete shock, not just to me but to most people, I think. But assaulting a police officer is a serious offence, so …' She shrugged. 'In a way, I'm actually grateful. I might not have come to my senses quite so fast if I hadn't ended up in jail. I've got 'the old me' back. And I'm going to be very careful who I fall for in the future, that's for sure.'

'Are you … planning on staying? Or are you going back to Spain?'

Sharp lines formed around Alexia's eyes and her lips wobbled slightly.

'I don't know. It depends on Dad.' Tears welled up in her eyes and she made no attempt to wipe them away. 'I … I think I'm the cause of his heart attack. I know I wasn't here, but I believe the shock of it all has been building. Dad keeps his real feelings close to his chest. We had a wonderful Christmas and New Year in Spain and Dad actually seemed quite excited at the prospect of retiring and moving out there permanently. But I believe it's because he thinks that's what Mum wants. She's always idolised me. Even after everything I said and did. If none of it had happened and we were all still jogging along as we were before I got involved with Tom, I'm fairly certain Dad's episode wouldn't have occurred.'

'You can't be sure of that. Heart attacks can strike at any time. And without warning. That I do know. At least he's alive. And Bear says he'll be fine. As long as he takes it easy for a while and doesn't do anything stupid.'

Alexia smiled before a horrified expression swept across her beautiful face. 'Oh my God, Mia! What's wrong with me? I haven't even mentioned Garrick. I'm so, so sorry about Fiona. It was such a shock when I heard. I can't begin to imagine how you must be feeling. And here's me going on about myself. I'm really sorry.'

Mia shook her head. 'It's okay. Even after almost a week, it hasn't fully sunk in yet. But thanks. Garrick's devastated, obviously. Ella's with him and his parents are there, of course. Fiona's mum has early onset Alzheimer's. She's had it for several years, and I never thought I'd say this, but it's almost a blessing in this case. She has no idea her only daughter has died. Fiona and Garrick did take baby Flora to meet her, apparently, but she's in stage seven, the final stage, and didn't have a clue who they were or even that they were there. She's bedridden and has a few other serious health problems besides. According to Ella, it's only a matter of days now, so the care home people say.' Tears appeared from nowhere and Mia swiped them away. 'Sorry. It's just all so bloody awful. That poor woman is dying and she doesn't know what's happened. Even if she lives until Fiona's funeral, she can't go.'

Alexia reached out for Mia's hand and squeezed it. 'Life can be cruel. It makes me realise how important it is to live it to the full because none of us knows what's waiting around the corner. When is the funeral? Are you going?'

Mia got up and grabbed a tissue from a box on the counter, sobbing even more. It took a few seconds to pull herself together.

'I don't understand the procedure in Scotland, but Ella said that the Procurator Fiscal or whatever he's called, is involved in cases where there may be a Fatal Accident Inquiry, or where criminal proceedings may be brought. He instructs a post mortem to be carried out and only once the cause of death is established and he has all the information he needs, will he release the body. He did that yesterday and signed the cremation certificate. The police have investigated and will be prosecuting the lorry driver. Although anyone could've told you that he was to blame. But red tape is red tape, no matter what, I suppose. Ella will let me know once they've got a date for the funeral. Garrick wants it to be small. He's not coping well and can't face a large affair.'

'It's so unbelievably sad. And now he's got a tiny baby to look after. Will he remain in Scotland? Aberdeen, isn't it? Or will he move back to London, near his parents? Unless he's thinking of coming back here. He'll need all the help he can get at such a time.'

For some absurd reason, Mia hadn't even thought about that. There was nothing to keep him in Scotland now. He could work from anywhere, as he proved when he lived in Sunbeam Cottage, so his business wasn't an issue. And Mia had already decided that she would help him as much as she could. Why not? She'd have to discuss it with Ella and Gill, of course. And possibly with Jet, although he would agree, she was sure because it made perfect sense.

Garrick should return to Little Pondale. To Lily Pond Lane. To Sunbeam Cottage. There was plenty of room. That way he would have all the help he could possibly need. Not just from his sister, but from Mia, too. And he'd be surrounded by family and friends and people who loved him. His parents could visit often; there was even room for them assuming baby Flora would be in a cot in Garrick's room. Or they could stay at Little Pond Farm.

It would take a while, obviously, but Garrick could start to rebuild his life. To make a future for himself and Flora.

And maybe, in time, he would fall in love again.

With someone new.

Why didn't that prospect please her quite as much as it should?

Chapter Seven

Ella was all for the idea when Mia called her that afternoon to suggest it, but thought perhaps, they should wait until after the funeral to mention it to Garrick.

'And there's something I need to tell you,' Ella added.

'Oh God. Not more bad news.' Mia took a deep breath and waited.

'Not exactly. It's about the funeral. We've just arranged it and it's going to be next Friday. But please don't get mad or feel hurt. The thing is, Garrick doesn't want you to come. Not only you. He doesn't want anyone there. Just me, Mum and Dad. And Flora. Fiona hated funerals, apparently. Not that she's the only one, is she?'

'Oh. Er. Okay. I'm not upset. I was dreading it. I'd probably stand there balling my eyes out and that wouldn't be good for anyone. And it's not as if Fiona and I were close or anything. I know she and Garrick originally dated for five years or so but I never felt as if I really knew her. And then what with Garrick and me last summer and everything. Well, I'm not sure Fiona would want me there either. So is that what she wanted? Just close family? No friends or anything?'

'Haven't a clue. They hadn't discussed it because neither of them thought they'd need to be talking about their own bloody funerals when they're in their thirties.'

'Who does?'

'Precisely. Oddly enough though, they did both make a will. But that was because of Flora.'

'I've got a will. Clive Dale kept nagging me to make one. David did it for me. Clive's son, remember? But I suppose I should make a new one now I'm engaged to Jet. It didn't even occur to me.'

'No point me having one. I've got nothing to leave. Anyway, Garrick said they went to someone else's funeral recently and Fiona said at the time that she didn't want one. That she simply wanted to be cremated and have her ashes scattered somewhere lovely. She didn't even care where. He doesn't know if that really is what she would've wanted but as that's the only thing he heard her say on the subject, that's the decision he's made. It's not as if he can ask her family. Other than her mum, who can't be any help, obviously, she didn't have any. I'm telling you now, Mia. If I die and Gill's not around, or we die together, I want the whole shebang. A big carriage pulled by four beautiful black horses. More flowers than you could fill a shop with and everyone crying and saying how wonderful I was and that life will never be the same without me. Oh, and I want my ashes to be scattered on the moon, or somewhere equally fabulous. With all your dosh, you can arrange that, right?' Ella laughed down the phone.

'Absolutely. And I'll arrange for a cannon to be fired, trumpets to be played and flags to be lowered, shall I? Life never will be the same without you, if you die before me. I can vouch for that. God. What an awful thought. I don't know what I want. The carriage and the horses, obviously. Oh no. The reindeer. And maybe a sleigh type of thing instead of a carriage. I'd quite like to have my ashes scattered on Frog Hill. Or in Frog's Hollow, near the pond.'

'What? So that you can watch everyone going skinny dipping on Midsummer's Eve? You dirty old bag!'

Mia gave a snort of laughter. 'No. So that Hettie Turner will tell everyone that my spirit haunts it and it's not just on a Monday that you should avoid the place. You should also avoid it on whatever day it is that I die.'

'Yeah. There's one minor flaw in your plan. As Hettie's in her eighties, she'll be long dead before you. Oh God. Unless … No. I'm not even going to say it. And I think we should change the subject. So, Alexia came grovelling, did she? Do you believe her? Or do you think she'll be up to her old tricks again the minute your back's turned?'

'I honestly don't know. She seemed so sincere. And there were genuine tears in her eyes when she mentioned her dad. Plus, she did bring the most beautiful bouquet. And a box of Jenny's cakes. The really expensive ones.'

'The ones with all the cream in the middle and the special icing and handmade decorations you mean?'

'Yep.'

'Damn. Why couldn't she have waited until I got back? Are you friends now then?'

'I wouldn't go as far as to say that. No. Let's just say we'll be polite to one another when we meet, but I won't be inviting her round for supper anytime soon. And speaking of supper, I'd better get to the shops or Jet won't be getting any when he gets back from rugby this afternoon.'

'Are we still talking about supper, or have we moved on to sex?'

Mia tutted. 'Don't you start. I've had enough of that from Alexia.'

'What, sex? And you're not even friends! I'm shocked.'

'Get lost and go and do something useful. Call me tomorrow.'

'I will. Oh, and if Garrick does agree to this idea of yours, you'd better start learning how to change a nappy and hold your nose at the same time. God, that stuff stinks. I thought babies smelt of vanilla or something lovely like that, not like every toilet in the known universe has exploded and landed in their nappy. Make sure you've got plenty of wine in. We're going to need it. Love you lots. Now I'm going to call Gill and tell him I won't be seeing him till next weekend.'

'Isn't he at rugby practice today?'

'Damn. I forgot. Oh! Didn't you say Alexia was back playing rugby? Keep her away from Gill, please. I don't want to come home and find my gorgeous boyfriend has fallen into her evil clutches.'

'But she's a changed woman, have you forgotten?' Mia emphasised the sarcasm in her voice.

'Yeah. And I'm Meghan, Duchess of Sussex. And I've really got to go now because Prince Harry wants his tea.'

Chapter Eight

Jet wasn't quite as keen on the idea of Garrick returning to Sunbeam Cottage as Mia assumed he would be. When she told him about it that evening, he choked on his Chicken Vindaloo. Mia's cooking skills weren't yet up to making curry from scratch, so she'd bought this one, freshly prepared at the supermarket. Quite how 'freshly prepared' it really was, was questionable, but Jet did like a curry and after all the terrible news, Mia decided they should have a treat. At first she thought he was choking because she'd got the one the supermarket had labelled 'Volcanic Vindaloo' and that it was too hot, even for Jet, who loved spicy food, but his next words – once he was able to speak without his eyes watering and his face turning red, showed it wasn't only the curry that was getting him hot under the collar.

'You're seriously suggesting that the man you were going to marry, before everyone discovered

Fiona was pregnant, and who is now a single dad of a pretty cute baby, as babies go, should come back and live in the cottage where, as everyone in the village also knows, you and he spent every night in the same bed for the entire summer. Is that right?' He maintained eye contact as he gulped down his beer.

'Ah. Well, when you put it like that, I can see why some people might feel it is a little inappropriate. But I'm living with you now and you're the one I love, so why should we care what anyone else thinks?'

'Really? That's your answer? It didn't occur to you that it might make me a bit uncomfortable?'

She blinked at him. 'Frankly no. That thought didn't even enter my head. Why would it? It's not as if you've got any reason to feel uncomfortable. And there's definitely no need to be concerned, or jealous, or anything. Garrick is merely a friend. A good friend. And he always will be. I thought you were okay with that.'

'When the guy was six hundred or so miles away in Scotland, living with his pretty girlfriend, the mother of his child ... yes. Not so much knowing that he may be living on our doorstep and is single again, with a cute kid in tow.'

'Jet! It's not his fault he's single again. Show the man some mercy. And that fact doesn't change my feelings towards him, and it shouldn't change yours. Are you honestly saying that you don't trust me?'

'No. Of course not. I trust you completely. I'm saying I'm not one hundred per cent certain I trust him.'

'I have to say I'm surprised. I honestly didn't think it would be an issue. But if that's how you genuinely feel then I'll tell Ella that we don't think it's such a good idea, after all.'

Jet put his glass on the table and sighed. 'You can't do that. Ella's probably already told him.'

'No. She was going to wait until after the funeral before suggesting it.'

'Ella? Wait to tell someone something? I doubt that very much. She'll tell him the first chance she gets.'

'She won't. I'll call her after supper and tell her.'

Jet sighed again and shook his head. 'No. Don't do that. Whether she has or hasn't told him, you're right. The guy's been through hell. He needs all the support we can give him. And I really like him. I just don't like the thought that he may not be completely over you.'

Mia beamed at him and tossed her hair coquettishly over her shoulder. 'Because I'm so hard to forget, you mean?'

'Absolutely, Margaret,' he joked.

'I'll give you Margaret, Jet Cross. It's lucky for you that I'm crazy about you.'

'Remember to tell Garrick that at least once a day. Preferably twice.' He sipped his beer and gazed lovingly at her over the rim of the glass.

'Are you really sure you're okay with it? I should've spoken to you before I mentioned it to Ella but I honestly didn't see it as a problem.'

'It's not. I'm being a jerk. This being madly in love and blissfully happy lark is still new to me. I haven't quite got to grips with the dynamics of it. But it's fine. And we could do with another man on the team. Garrick was a good player.'

'Re-joining the rugby team will probably be the last thing on his mind. Ella says he's not coping well at all.'

'I'm sorry he's struggling. But believe me, he'll want to play. And it'll be cathartic for him. He can let out some of his anger and frustration on the field. I'm just glad he'll be on my team.' He grinned and glanced at the landline phone as its ring interrupted him. 'I bet that's Ella.'

'Nope. She's going to call tomorrow.'

Jet got up to answer it and his grin broadened as he raised his brows. 'Hi Ella. We were just talking about you.'

'Smart-arse,' Mia said, taking the phone he held out to her. And five minutes later, when she hung up, she pulled a face and poured herself another glass of wine. 'Okay. So you were right. Ella's told Garrick.'

Jet grinned harder. 'And?'

'And I'd like to wipe that cocky smile off your face, mister, but it seems you were right about the rugby thing too. She said Garrick wasn't sure it was such a good idea at first but their dad reminded him of all the things he enjoyed down here and as soon as rugby was mentioned, Garrick's face lit up for the first time since this nightmare happened. She couldn't believe it. And then he started talking about the beach and the fact that Flora would be safe because there were very few cars in the village and no lorry ever comes through it.'

Jet shook his head, the grin gone from his face and replaced by genuine sympathy.

'Rugby will help, and so will having friends around him, but it's going to take the poor guy a long time to get over this.'

'And you're sure you're okay about it?'

He got to his feet and walked to where Mia was leaning against the counter. Taking her in his arms, he smiled and nodded. 'Yes.'

'Then I'd better learn how to change a nappy.' She slid her arms around him and pulled him close.

'And how to deal with the temper tantrums, crying, sulking and demands for cuddles and constant attention.'

'It's a bit too soon for that. Flora's still only three weeks old.'

He tilted his head to one side, his mouth just inches from hers. 'I wasn't talking about Flora. I was talking about me.' And he kissed the laughter from her lips.

Chapter Nine

The next morning a bout of snow arrived and although Mia loved snow, it did make things more difficult on the farm. The chickens, for one thing, weren't so keen to range freely when a carpet of white rubbed against their stomachs. Not that Mia went near them if she could help it. Those, she left to Jet, Franklin or Pete to deal with. The reindeer, however, couldn't wait to get out in it, or so it seemed. Three of them tried to squeeze out of the barn before Mia had a chance to open the door more than six inches. She nearly landed on her bottom. Jet had told her, more than once, to stand to one side as she opened it but yet again she stood in front, and risked being trampled. Thank goodness there were only four of them and they had the good manners to walk around her.

Mia helped out on the farm all morning and early afternoon. Later, she scanned the internet for tips on looking after babies, while cooking dinner and baking a couple of cakes for her pantry. She loved having a pantry. It made her feel like Nigella Lawson – although Mia was far from being a domestic goddess. Sometimes, it was difficult to decide whether to ice her cakes, or use them as stepping stones in her soon-to-be, herb and vegetable garden. Looking after babies might prove equally taxing from what she'd read so far.

'How did you do it, Mum?' she asked Lori, over coffee the following day. The snow had stopped but a few centimetres covered the ground and more was forecast for that day.

Lori shrugged. 'I'm not really sure. It was mainly trial and error, I think. We just got on with it. When it's your own child, it seems to come naturally, but if it doesn't, you have to learn as you go along.'

That wasn't very helpful. And neither was Hettie when Mia popped into her cottage to see if she or Fred needed anything from the shops. They didn't, but Hettie insisted that Mia stop for a cup of tea and when they got to baby advice, Hettie had none to give.

'As you discovered at Christmas, I couldn't have children so I haven't got any more idea than you, deary.'

Mia nodded. 'Speaking of that. How are things going with Leo? Does he still visit you to talk about his dad?'

Hettie beamed, leant back against the sofa and crossed her chubby arms beneath her chest. 'He does. Leo's a wonderful man and Hector would've been immensely proud. Cathy and Daisy come with Leo sometimes too. It almost feels as if he's my own son, you know, deary. Like I've got my own little family. Chatting about Hector again is bringing me such joy. And Fred doesn't mind a bit. I'm very lucky, deary. Oh. I hear young Garrick's moving back. How does our dear Jet feel about that?'

'He's fine with it. Why wouldn't he be? Fred doesn't mind you talking about Hector. Why would Jet mind Garrick moving back?'

Hettie's surprise was evident. Mia hadn't meant to snap.

'Well for one thing, deary, my Hector's dead and has been for many a year. Although as you know, he didn't leave me completely until I married Fred, and Hector had to move on to his next life. For another, being with me from the spirit world isn't quite the same as being with someone in the real world, is it? Personally, deary, I would be surprised if Jet wasn't just a little anxious about it. You were engaged to Garrick after all and you did share a bed for several months. And we all know how much Garrick loved you.'

Mia sighed. 'You're right. But I didn't lie. Jet was a bit put out at first, but now he's okay with it. Honestly. And I'd better go. I told him I'd only be an hour and I've been here for longer than that. By the time I get to the shops, he'll think I've got lost in a snow drift or something.' The predicted snow for that day hadn't yet arrived and the layer on the ground was rapidly turning to ice but as Mia got up and glanced out of the window, the clouds looked fit to burst. The wind was also picking up and branches swayed and swirled as it tugged at them.

'At least he won't think you've run away with Garrick.' Hettie's bosom heaved with laughter. 'Well not yet, anyway, deary.'

'That's not funny, Hettie.'

'No. I'm sorry, my dear. It was only a joke but a very bad one, I'll admit. Why don't you give the lovely lad a quick call from here, and let him know you're running late?'

Mia did as Hettie suggested but as she drove to the shops, which in this weather took much longer than the usual half an hour or so to reach, she kept wondering if Garrick moving back to the village was such a good thing, after all.

Would everyone be watching her and Garrick to see if there was still a spark of attraction? Would she have to call Jet and tell him where she was if she was late, just to make sure he didn't think she was with Garrick? Would everyone in the pub be taking bets on a 'will they, won't they scenario'? Although since all that upset last year, Freda had promised never to do anything like that again, and Alec may be out of hospital today, but he still wasn't up to helping out in the pub, so he wouldn't be acting as a bookie.

Another thing was niggling at Mia as the predicted snow arrived, her wipers struggling to cope with the sudden heavy drifts caused by increasing winds from the north-east. She hadn't seen Garrick since he left with Fiona last September. Not in the flesh at least. And they'd only chatted via Skype a couple of times since Christmas. It had taken Garrick longer to deal with their break-up than it had taken her. How would they feel when they saw each other again? Would they hug? Would they kiss as they always had before she and Garrick became lovers? Or would they simply smile, say hello, and keep their distance?

She couldn't get it off her mind and shopping took much longer because she kept forgetting what she needed and had to go back to several aisles for items she had missed. The only reason she was shopping now was because she had forgotten half the things she wanted on her shopping trip on Saturday. She really needed to stop thinking about Garrick and concentrate on the task at hand. But by the time she drove out of the car park there was several centimetres of snow on the tarmac, and visibility was getting worse by the minute.

Perhaps she should wait and see if conditions improved? But what if they grew worse? The journey usually took thirty minutes or so but in this weather it would take far longer. The roads had been gritted and thankfully, there wasn't that much traffic but Mia made sure to drive as carefully as she could. She didn't want to go too slow though or she might end up stranded, like all those cars and lorries she had seen on the TV the last time they had a blizzard like this.

A car horn blared and she swerved to try to avoid a collision, but in spite of the grit, in such dreadful conditions her tyres wouldn't grip and she skidded on the ice and freshly fallen snow.

Everything seemed to happen in slow motion. An image of Fiona walking along the road and turning just as headlights bore down, popped into Mia's head, followed by Garrick pacing a hospital corridor and blaming himself for not offering to go to the shop; Jet standing at the top of Frog Hill, sprinkling something from an urn and cursing himself for not telling Mia to come home instead of going on to the shops knowing such awful weather had been forecast.

I'm going to die, Mia thought, before everything went black as her car ploughed head-first into a bank of deep and heavy snow.

Chapter Ten

'What in God's name happened?'

Mia's head was pounding, and Jet demanding answers wasn't helping one bit. She tried to sit up. 'You're hurting my hand, Jet.'

He looked mortified and quickly let go, jumping off the edge of the hospital bed. 'I'm sorry.' He paced the small, private room. 'But I need to know.'

'And if I knew, I'd tell you. All I can remember is visibility getting worse and suddenly not being able to see, then a car horn blaring and me heading into a bank of white. Or possibly black because that was the colour I saw as I hit my head. But I'm fine. Apart from this headache and my legs aching. Oh God. My legs are okay, aren't they?' She lifted the sheet, wiggled her toes and moved her legs from side to side but apart from some vivid purple bruises, they seemed fine.

Jet frowned and came back to the bedside. 'You may have a concussion. You're being kept in overnight, but considering the car's a write-off, according to the police, you had a miraculous escape.'

'Oh great! Hospital food. Wait. What? The car's a write-off? Damn. It was brand new.'

'This isn't funny. I nearly died when Lori called me. Her name was on a card in your purse as your contact in case of an accident so they called her, and she called me. Jesus, Mia. After what happened to Fiona, can you imagine what went through my head? And through Lori's?'

Mia closed her eyes for one second and screwed up her face. 'I'm sorry. It must've been awful for you both. But I didn't do it on purpose.'

He shook his head and smiled lovingly. 'I know that. All I'm saying is … actually, I don't know what I'm saying. But I do know a little of how Garrick's feeling. All I could think about was that when you called me from Hettie's I should've told you not to go to the shops because of the forecast and that it was so late in the day.'

Mia opened her eyes wide. 'I knew you'd be thinking that. I saw an image of you saying it. Only you were sprinkling what looked worryingly like my ashes. I'm not dead am I and dreaming this?' She glanced around the room and banged her hand on the cabinet beside her to be sure.

'No, thank God.'

'And the other person who blared their horn at me? The one in the car I had to swerve to avoid? Are they okay?'

'Unhurt. They think. He didn't stop. But it wasn't that guy whose horn you heard. It was a woman in the car behind his. The police suspect the driver of the car you avoided was either over the limit, on drugs, or had fallen asleep at the wheel. He'd drifted onto your side of the road. Fortunately, you got out of his way and skidded into a bank of snow. If it hadn't been snowing so heavily, you might've sustained serious injuries because there was a brick wall behind that bank of snow. The woman in the car behind called the emergency services.'

Mia saw the look of dread on his face and smiled. 'It's a bit like the chicken and the egg, isn't it? If not for the snow I might be worse off, but if it hadn't been snowing, visibility wouldn't have been so bad, I would've seen the guy coming, and I wouldn't have skidded into the bank of snow. But I'm fine. That's all that matters, isn't it? Not even a cut on my forehead. Where's Mum? You said they called her. Didn't she come?'

'Of course she came,' Lori's voice boomed out as she hurried into the room. 'I went to the loo, and to call Franklin to tell him you're going to be okay. We've all been worried sick about you.' She went to Mia and hugged her tight, a tear or two rolling down her cheeks. 'Oh my darling, I could've lost you. It doesn't bear thinking about.

Even the doctors are amazed you'll walk away tomorrow and that the X-rays showed there's no internal damage. Are you really okay? Do you want anything? Are you in pain?'

Mia smiled and eased her mum away. 'My head hurts and my legs ache but other than that I'm fine.' She glanced from Lori to Jet, serious now. 'It's weird though, isn't it?'

They both frowned, glanced at one another and simultaneously said: 'What?'

'The accident. Fiona was killed because a lorry driver lost control when she was headed to the shop. Don't you see the similarity? I was going to the shops. It was snowing heavily, just like it was the day she died. Someone lost control of their vehicle.' She shivered as she said it.

Jet and Lori exchanged glances once again.

'Yes,' Lori said. 'That is rather peculiar. Are you saying that in some strange way, your Fate and Fiona's may be linked?'

'No,' Jet said, emphatically. 'There are hundreds of accidents like this every day, especially since we've been having such heavy snowfalls on and off over the last two months. The guy who nearly hit you was probably drunk, and didn't stop. The lorry driver wasn't. He was using his mobile phone. Please don't start seeing things that aren't there. Don't you think we've had enough to worry about?'

'Jet's right,' Lori said, standing up and patting Mia's hand. 'Shall I get you some coffee?'

'Yes, please. That would be great. My throat feels like the inside of the chicken shed.'

Jet grinned. 'I'm surprised you can remember what the inside of the chicken shed's like. You haven't been inside their barn for weeks. I'll get the coffee, Lori.' He winked at Mia. 'I love you, Mia, but I think you should know that I'm not letting you out of my sight for the foreseeable future. Apart from right now. To get your coffee.'

'I love you, too. And that's fine with me. I'll be by your side day and night, apart from when you milk the cows or feed the chickens.'

He laughed as he turned away, but stopped and gave her a serious look over his shoulder. 'I don't know what I'd do without you, Mia. I know it wasn't your fault, but please don't ever scare me like this again.' And then he disappeared into the corridor.

'That man adores you, darling,' Lori said, perching herself on the edge of the bed. 'And you adore him. Don't ever forget that.'

'Why would I forget it, Mum? That's a strange thing to say.'

'Maybe. But when I got the call about your accident, the policewoman said she wasn't sure if there was someone else she should've called, like a husband, or partner, or someone because when the rescue services first got you out of the car, you kept repeating two names over and over again. One was Jet. The other one was Garrick.'

Chapter Eleven

The January snow melted into February and life in Little Pondale slowly returned to normal. Mia had suffered no ill effects after her crash – unless you counted a few more restless nights and bad dreams, all of which Jet helped her through, either with reassuring words or passionate kisses. She really was the luckiest girl in the world. A pronouncement that held more resonance after she saw photos of her crash and her battered car that had been posted on social media, and printed in the local papers.

Since coming home from hospital, she hadn't left Little Pond Farm. Neither she nor Jet wanted to be out of each other's sight, and as he had a farm to run, Mia stayed in the farmhouse. Not quite by his side as she had said, but close enough. She had ventured out into the farmyard once or twice, or the fields to see the reindeer, but on those occasions, Jet actually was by her side.

'Alec's growing stronger by the day,' Gill said. He'd popped into Little Pond Farm to buy some cheese, and to check on Mia, which he'd done each day after she came home on Tuesday, so that he could reassure Ella that her best friend was fine. Ella had even insisted on daily photos, just to be sure. 'Last night he showed his face behind the bar. Just showed his face though, before Freda demanded to know what the devil he thought he was doing and told him in no uncertain terms to get back in his chair and put his feet up. She, Toby, Alexia and Christy are making sure no customer has to wait longer than a minute or two for their drinks and not much longer than that for their food orders. Christy's been welcomed by all the Bywaters with open arms, including Alexia you'll be pleased to hear, and has now become a full-time member of staff.'

'I'm glad,' Mia said, grinning at the image of Freda giving Alec orders. 'But I suppose my suggestion that Christy could move in has had to be put on hold. Now that we don't know whether Freda and Alec are staying or going, and due to the fact that Alexia's returned.'

Gill nodded. 'Yeah. But Toby says his dad's still adamant about moving to Spain if Alexia decides to go back, so we'll have to wait and see. He sends his love by the way. They all do.'

'Thanks. Everyone's been so kind. Popping in all the time, or sending flowers, chocolates and, in Jenny's case, bringing me loads of delicious cakes.

At this rate I'll be as fat as an elephant by the time Ella comes home tomorrow. I don't think I've moved at all in the four days since getting home from hospital.'

Gill laughed before a look of sadness crept over his handsome face. He took off his glasses and wiped the lenses. 'I can't believe how much I've missed her. The cottage is so quiet without her there. But on the upside, I've got a lot of writing done.' He put his glasses back on and smiled.

'I've missed her too. I'm really looking forward to seeing her. We've Skyped one another of course, but it isn't the same, is it?'

'No, it isn't.' He drank his coffee. 'Oh. Did you hear that the entire village is breathing a collective sigh of relief because you had your accident?'

'No. Why? They don't want me bumped off or something, do they?'

Gill laughed heartily. 'Don't be daft. Everyone in Little Pondale loves you. It's because of Hettie. After Alec and Fiona, she told everyone that bad things come in threes. She told us that, remember? At first she thought the third bad thing was Alexia returning. That made Alexia chortle, as you can imagine.' He raised his brows and shook his head. 'Why someone hasn't done away with Hettie is beyond me. Anyway. She's now telling everyone that she was wrong, and that your accident last week was clearly the third bad thing, so we can all get on with our lives without a care in the world. Or some such nonsense.'

'Oh good. I'm so glad to have been of service. Want some more coffee?'

'No thanks. I'd better be off. I need to get as much writing done as I can before Ella comes home tomorrow.' His eyes lit up as he got to his feet and a broad smile spread across his face. 'I think I'll be otherwise occupied for quite some time.'

'Lucky Ella.' Mia giggled as she knew precisely what Gill meant. 'Gill? You don't mind Garrick and Flora coming to stay, do you?'

'Not in the least. But if I'm completely honest, I'm not sure I'll feel the same if Flora cries all night. But Ella says she sleeps through most nights.' His smile turned into a wicked grin and he winked at Mia. 'And the baby does too. So we should all be fine. I thought babies needed regular feeds. But what do I know?'

Mia laughed. 'I know nothing about babies, so don't ask me. But Ella's like Jet. They can both sleep through a hurricane. Although funnily enough, since I've been having my bad dreams, do you know what? Jet's awake like a flash. Mum says it's some kind of sixth sense. When someone you care about is worried, or ill, or anything at all really, you instinctively know and are wide awake and ready for action.' She blushed at the thought of just how ready for action Jet always seemed to be, but kept that to herself. She'd told Ella, naturally, but some things you didn't share with your best friend's boyfriend.

Chapter Twelve

Mia wasn't sure what to do on the day Garrick returned to the cottage on Lily Pond Lane. So much had happened in less than a year. It was crazy. She wanted to see Ella, and was almost as eager to meet baby Flora in the flesh, and of course she wanted to see Garrick, give him a hug and tell him she was there for him and always would be. Except she wasn't. Not totally. She was with Jet.

In the end, it was Jet who made up her mind for her.

'I think we should be there when he arrives,' Jet said. 'Show him our support, tell him to call us if he needs anything at all, but give him his breathing space. Undoubtedly, Hettie will make her presence known, and Glen told Gill that, as the local vicar, he feels he should introduce himself in case Garrick needs him. Although he probably won't do that today. Glen's a good guy. He'll know the right time. If I were in Garrick's shoes,

I'd want to be left alone to settle in and then start seeing people in my own good time, not have everyone land on the doorstep the minute I arrive.'

'That makes sense,' Mia said. 'Perhaps we should drop into Hettie and Fred on the way, and suggest she leaves it for a day or two.'

Which is exactly what they did.

When Garrick, Ella and baby Flora pulled into the drive of Sunbeam Cottage in Garrick's van, most of Garrick's belongings piled in the back, it reminded Mia of that day last May when she, Ella and Garrick first arrived in Little Pondale; he in his van, following behind Mia and Ella in Mia's old car. Except no one had been on the doorstep to greet them.

At the time, she'd seen it as a fresh start, a new beginning, not just for her but for Ella and Garrick too. And boy what an adventure they'd all been on. More so in Mia's case. Discovering all Mattie's secrets. Well, most of them. Even now, Mia felt there might be more things still waiting to be uncovered as far as great-aunt Matilda was concerned. Falling in love; falling out of love; inheriting a fortune; meeting the man of her dreams; getting engaged. Twice. Making so many new friends, and finally finding out where her future truly lay. With Jet. She often felt she had been searching for Jet her entire life and at the age of thirty-three, she'd found him.

But why was she thinking about such things now? Garrick was getting out of the van.

It was as if his eyes automatically focused on her, and for a moment, he stood in the drive, staring at her.

Until Ella tumbled out of the passenger seat and screamed at the top of her lungs: 'We're here!'

Gill ambled towards her. 'Really? We hadn't noticed.' Then both he and Ella burst into a run and fell into each other's arms. 'I've missed you so much,' he said between kisses.

'I've only missed you about one hundred times each day,' Ella replied. 'We're going to have so much sex, you do realise that, don't you?' She stopped suddenly. 'Oh God. I'm sorry, Garrick. This is pretty tactless, isn't it?' She eased herself from Gill's embrace.

'Don't mind me,' Garrick said, his voice surprisingly calm. 'Make the most of every opportunity. You don't know when it might be your last.' He leant inside the van, fiddled with the seatbelt in the middle, and returned to full view with a bassinet in his hands. 'It's good to see you, Mia. And you, Jet. How are you?' He walked towards them, a friendly smile on his lips. 'Would you like to say hello to Flora?'

'Yes please,' Mia said, unable to contain the excitement in her voice. 'I've been dying to meet her. Oh no! I don't mean dying. I mean. Er.' She glanced at Jet for help but Garrick put her at ease.

'Please don't worry. I know what you meant. Don't feel you need to be careful what you say around me. It happened. It was the worst day of my life, but life goes on and eventually, I'll get over it. Or at least, come to terms with it. Dad says we need to face these things head-on, not try to hide from them and pretend it hasn't happened. Grief needs to be let out, not pent up inside. I may cry sometimes, or turn into a gibbering idiot, or dissolve into a puddle of helpless goo on the floor, but I don't want any of you to act any differently around me, okay? I need to be strong, if not for me then for Flora.'

Mia and Jet exchanged anxious glances.

'Okay,' Jet said. 'But we're here for you, you know that, don't you? No matter what. For you and for Flora.'

'Absolutely,' Mia added, peering into the bassinet as Garrick reached the doorstep.

'Thanks. That means a lot. And thanks for letting me come back here.' He met Mia's eyes as she glanced from Flora to him. 'I wasn't sure at first, but I think this is the best place I could be right now.'

'You'll always be welcome here.' Mia returned her gaze to Flora and reached inside to move the edge of a pale pink blanket from the baby's chin in order to get a better look at Flora's face. 'She's beautiful, Garrick.'

'She is,' added Jet, peering over Mia's shoulder.

'She takes after her mum,' Garrick said, a slight break in his voice. 'She'll definitely have Fiona's hair. You can see a few strands of red coming through amongst the tiny shock of brown. And she's got Fiona's eyes.'

'No. She's got your eyes, Garrick,' Mia said. 'And your mouth too. She's going to be a real stunner.'

'We should get her inside,' Jet said, a little sharply. 'It's freezing out here. We made a pot of coffee about five minutes ago. Unless you'd prefer a beer?'

'I could murder a beer,' Garrick said. 'But until I know this little one is settled, I'd better not. You're right though. She needs to be inside.'

There wasn't a trace of the snow, now but the days were bitterly cold and the nights, even more so and today was one of the coldest for some time. Mia and Jet stepped aside to let Garrick in, and Ella and Gill, who had been kissing again, hurried towards the door.

'There's a fire in the sitting room,' Mia said. 'Take Flora in there and I'll bring the coffee.'

'I'll get your things from the van,' Jet offered.

'Thanks,' Garrick said. 'That would be great. I'll put the bassinet down and come and give you a hand.'

'No you won't. I can manage. Besides, Gill can help.'

'What?' Gill looked as if he hadn't heard a word other than his name.

Ella smiled lovingly. 'Will you help Jet get our stuff while we go and get some coffee? I'm gasping.' She winked at him. 'And not just for coffee. So don't take too long.'

Gill grinned. 'I'm on it.'

Garrick headed into the sitting room and after Ella gave Mia the biggest hug imaginable, she dashed towards the loo. 'I also need to pee.'

'Thanks for sharing.' Mia laughed as she watched Ella run along the hall. 'God, I've missed you woman.'

'Backatcha,' Ella yelled.

Mia turned, and gasped as Garrick was standing right behind her. She took a small step back, hoping he wouldn't notice.

'I've missed you too,' he said. 'It's so good to be back here. But it's also a little weird. The last time I was here we...' His voice trailed off, but his eyes held her gaze.

'I know.' She tried to look away but couldn't.

'It feels like a lifetime ago. And yet, seeing you standing there, it feels like only yesterday.'

'I'm so sorry about Fiona, Garrick. Truly I am.' She had to change the subject.

'I know you are. But at least one of us is happy. You and Jet are engaged. Have you set a date yet?'

'No.' Mia shook her head. 'But we will. And soon, I expect.'

He stepped closer. 'When Ella told me about your accident on Monday, I nearly died for a second time in the space of just a couple of weeks. Are you really okay? I wanted to call, but I didn't know what to say. All I wanted was to shout at you. That's ridiculous, I know, but I was so angry. God, Mia. I could've lost you too. I couldn't bear the thought of that.'

What was he saying? Mia wasn't sure she liked where this might be heading. But he was still in shock, she must remember that. And coming back here had brought up their shared past – for both of them, so she couldn't blame him. But she had to make it clear she was in love with Jet. Deeply in love.

'That's exactly how Jet felt. And he did shout at me.' She tried to laugh but it came out like a cough. 'I didn't do it on purpose though. And I've promised him I won't do it again.'

Something flickered across his eyes but it was gone in a second and he smiled. 'That's good to know. I can breathe easy on that account then. But are you really okay? It's only been a few days.'

She nodded. 'Yes. I'm absolutely fine. A miraculous escape, apparently.'

A tiny gurgle from the bassinet commanded Garrick's full attention. He hurried to the sofa where he'd placed the wicker basket, looked inside and reached in for his child. He raised her gently and tenderly out from her blankets and cradled her in his arms. 'Daddy's here, my darling. You're safe and sound.'

As he kissed Flora on her delicate, rosy cheek, it looked as if Flora raised her tiny hand to touch his face and Mia felt as if her ovaries had exploded. A surge shot through her and if she hadn't known better she would have sworn her womb did a somersault followed by a backflip.

'She's awake?' Ella asked, coming in from the hall, just as Jet and Gill brought the first load in from the van.

'Where do you want your stuff?' Jet asked, glancing from Garrick to Mia and back again.

'Follow me,' Ella said. 'I asked Gill to put you in the old room you had when you lived here, Garrick. Not Mia's old room, of course. The one you had before you … um … this way.'

Clearly realising what she was about to say, Ella had stopped herself. Wow. There was a first time for everything. Mia smiled at her. 'I'll get that coffee.' She edged past Jet, who was blocking half the hall and gave him a quick kiss on his shoulder. He smiled at her in return.

'I'll have a beer, please,' he said.

'So will I,' said Gill.

'Me too,' said Garrick, still cradling Flora in his arms. 'I don't think Flora will mind.'

'Wine for me,' Ella said.

Jet, Gill, Garrick and Mia instantly made loud whiny noises, and in that moment, it felt like old times.

'Oh, ha ha,' Ella said.

They all burst out laughing as the fire in the sitting room crackled in the hearth and Mia inwardly breathed a sigh of relief. It was right that

Garrick was here. He was amongst good friends and his family.

Mia continued towards the kitchen while the others went upstairs, leaving Garrick and Flora to relax. Mia heard him trying to explain the joke to his four-week-old child and smiled. Perhaps she had nothing to worry about, after all. It may take a while and there might be a few hiccups along the way, but if just now was anything to go by, Garrick would soon settle in and find his own true future.

With someone else.

For some absurd reason, Mia suddenly remembered what that fortune-teller had told Garrick last summer. Or most of it, at least. She could almost hear Garrick saying it when he'd finally told them what the woman had said.

'She said I'd met the woman of my dreams and that we'll have a lifetime of happiness together with a large family. But that she saw two women in my life. One past, one present. Present could be past and past could be present. That she heard a child's heartbeat. That I had to make a choice and it would be the hardest one in my life so far. She saw a wedding and the saying "marry in haste, repent at leisure" would not apply. If I married in haste, I would find true pleasure. True happiness ... providing I made the right choice.'

Mia had thought it all made sense, especially when Fiona had reappeared. But now? The only parts that rang true were the hard choice and the child.

Why had Mia remembered it in so much detail? And why on earth had what that fortune-teller said, popped into her head right now?

Chapter Thirteen

Mia couldn't get that damn fortune-teller's words off her mind and, a few days later, when she, Ella and Lori were spending the evening together at Sunbeam Cottage, babysitting Flora while Garrick joined Jet, Gill and Franklin at rugby practice, she blurted it out to them.

'The fortune-teller?' Lori repeated, clearly astonished that Mia had brought that up after such a long time. 'How can you recall what she told Garrick, darling? I can hardly remember what she told me. Actually, that's not true. I think I can.'

'I can remember mine.' Ella topped up their wine glasses despite the fact that Mia had heard her promise Garrick earlier that they wouldn't have more than one glass of wine each. 'And everything she said has come true so far. Even the Swan Lake bit. I was only telling Fiona all about that the week before she died. And how wonderful the ballet was Gill took us to.'

'And I can remember mine,' Mia added, shaking her head as a wave of sadness swept over her at the mention of Fiona. 'And the other day, what the woman told Garrick came back to me. Don't ask me why but it did.'

'So what did she say?' Lori asked. 'Because I really can't remember his.'

'She said he'd met the woman of his dreams and that they'd have a lifetime of happiness together with a large family. But she saw two women in his life. One past, one present but that present could be past and past could be present. That she heard a child's heartbeat. That he had to make a choice and it would be the hardest of his life so far. She saw a wedding and the saying "marry in haste, repent at leisure" wouldn't apply. If he married in haste, he would find true pleasure. True happiness ... providing he made the right choice.'

'The baby bit was right,' Ella said. 'And the hard choice.'

'Exactly. But the rest of it can't possibly come true now, can it? We all assumed the two women were me and Fiona, and that one of us was "the woman of his dreams". Fiona, obviously, because he went back to her, but now? Well, he can't marry either of us, can he? In haste or otherwise.'

Ella grinned. 'He could still marry you if you dumped Jet.'

'That's not going to happen.'

'Okay. No need to bite my head off. It was a joke. Obviously, you're not going to dump Jet for my brother.'

'Sorry. Since my accident I've got a bit cranky.' Mia blew Ella a kiss.

'Don't blame the accident, honey. You were cranky long before you drove your car into a pile of snow.' Ella blew a kiss back.

'Perhaps the two women *were* you and Fiona,' Lori said. 'But that doesn't necessarily mean that either of you are "the woman of his dreams", darling.'

'What?' Mia looked from her mum to Ella and back.

'Oh, I see,' said Ella, almost spilling her wine as she curled her feet beneath her. 'What you're saying is that those sentences, or predictions or whatever, weren't connected?'

'That's right.' Lori leant forward to check on Flora who was sleeping in the bassinet safely positioned between her and Ella on the sofa, before smiling at Mia seated on the armchair opposite.

'What?' Mia said again.

Ella tutted. 'He might've met the woman of his dreams years ago and she's got nothing to do with you or Fiona.'

'And if that's the case,' Lori said, 'the rest of the prediction could still come true. They could meet up again, fall madly in love and decide to get married within a matter of months.'

'Or weeks,' Ella said. 'She did say "haste", after all.'

'I see.' Knowing that the woman of Garrick's dreams was out there somewhere, waiting to find him again didn't exactly fill Mia with joy, even though she wanted nothing more than for Garrick to be happy.

'Honey, we're home,' Gill's voice rang out from the doorway.

'Is it ten already?' Ella said, glancing towards the clock.

Gill, Garrick and Franklin tumbled into the sitting room, shoving and pushing one another as if they were still on the rugby field but Garrick's smile slid from his face when he saw the two empty wine bottles standing on the coffee table.

'One glass, you promised.' He glared at Ella as he strode towards the bassinet and peered inside.

'Mum and I drank most of it,' Mia lied, which resulted in shocked expressions from both Lori and Franklin.

'Yes,' Lori said. 'I'm still recovering from the shock of nearly losing my darling daughter. Oh gosh. I'm sorry, Garrick.'

He gave her a wan smile. 'It's fine, Lori. I'm just glad to know that my dear sister takes the care of her niece seriously enough to abstain from drinking far too much.'

'I do. Honestly. And I promise I'll curb my drinking whenever I'm looking after her.'

'Er. Where's Jet?' Mia craned her neck to peer into the hall but there was no sign of him. 'He didn't go home without me, did he?'

'No. He's walking Jenny home,' Gill said. 'He'll be here in a sec. Glen's at some religious shindig today and won't be back till tomorrow so Jenny popped into the pub for a pint.'

'Oh.' Mia breathed a sigh of relief. 'If we'd known that, we could've asked her to join us.'

'Are you drunk?' Ella asked Gill, grinning at him.

'I believe I am. A little.'

Franklin laughed. 'Alexia wagered she could score more drop goals. And the little lady won.'

Garrick added: 'The bet was that the loser had to down a shot of tequila equivalent to the number of goals they lost by. Let's just say that Gill says he wasn't on his best form tonight. Alexia on the other hand, was at her peak.'

'It's so good to have the lovely Alexia back in the fold, isn't it?' Ella said, her voice dripping with sarcasm as she got up from the sofa and Garrick took her place. 'Come on then. I'd better get you to bed.'

'I like the sound of that,' Gill said, a broad grin on his lips. 'And I bet I can get upstairs before you.' He spun round on one leg and shot forward, bashing his forehead against the side of the sitting room door.

'Good luck with that,' said Ella, tutting as she raised her eyebrows and exchanged a knowing look with Mia before grabbing Gill by the arm.

Franklin slapped him on the back before smiling at Lori. 'We'd best hit the hay, darlin'. I've got a real early start tomorrow.'

Lori got up from the sofa, kissed the tip of one finger and gently touched it against the tip of Flora's tiny upturned nose. 'I'll see you soon, little angel. Good night Garrick.' She kissed Mia's cheek. 'Sleep well, sweetheart. I'll see you for coffee tomorrow.'

'Night all.' Franklin tipped the Stetson he always wore and with one arm around Lori, they left Mia and Garrick alone.

'I'll wait outside for Jet,' Mia said, getting to her feet.

'Don't be silly. You can wait in the warm. He won't be long.'

'I don't want to keep you up.'

'Don't worry about me. I hardly sleep these days anyway. I suppose I should say, nights.'

'Because of Flora? I thought Ella said the baby slept through most nights.'

Garrick gave a small laugh. 'Ella sleeps through most nights. Babies need feeding every few hours at this age. But Flora's no trouble at all. She sometimes goes for four hours at a time between feeds. The reason I'm not sleeping is because of Fiona. Amongst other things.'

'Four hours? You have to get up every four hours? Blimey. I'm not sure I want to be a mum. Wait. Other things? Like what?'

'Like you.'

Their eyes met and held but Jet appeared in the doorway before Mia could respond, or Garrick could elaborate. Garrick looked away and focused his attention on Flora while Mia smiled at Jet, hoping that the heat she felt in her cheeks wasn't apparent on her face. She always blushed when she felt guilty about something. Although right now, she had absolutely nothing to feel guilty about.

Did she?

The look in Jet's eyes told her he might be wondering the same thing.

'Jenny home safe and sound?' Mia asked, walking towards the door but before Jet could answer, she turned to Garrick. 'Good night, Garrick. We'll let ourselves out.'

Jet and Garrick nodded to one another and said a brief 'Good night.' Then Jet walked ahead of Mia and opened the front door.

'That looked cosy,' he said, closing the door behind them as they stepped into the bitter night air.

'That room always does.' Mia linked her arm through his.

'That's not what I meant and you know it.' His voice was calm but there was a definite undercurrent.

'I have no idea what you're talking about. If you mean the fact that Garrick and I were alone when you arrived, I hate to disappoint you, but Mum and Franklin left about five seconds before you arrived. You must've seen them.'

'I did. It wasn't the fact you were alone. It was the look he was giving you.'

Mia stopped and looked him in the eye. 'What look?'

'The kind of look a guy gives a girl when he wants her.'

Her mouth fell open. 'Don't be so bloody ridiculous. I don't know what's going on with you, Jet Cross, but I never had you down as a jealous and possessive control freak.' She yanked her arm from his and glared at him. She wasn't sure why she was so cross. Was it with him? Or with Garrick? He glared back and they stood at the end of the drive for a good few seconds with neither one speaking.

'I'm sorry.' He reached out for her and gently placed his hands on her arms, his voice full of remorse. 'You're right. I'm being a jerk. I don't know what's going on with me either. Ever since Fiona died, I've felt as if I'm tilting on the edge of a precipice. I know I said your dreams were nothing, but I think, in some small way, they freaked me out a bit too. Then you had your accident and my head exploded and my brain turned to mush. At least that's what it felt like. It's crazy. It really is. I don't believe in this stuff, normally, but … I sort of get the feeling that this isn't over. The bad things happening, I mean. Does that sound mad?'

Mia leant against him and he slid his arms around her. 'No. It doesn't sound mad at all. Because I feel the same.' She lifted her face to look him in the eye.

'Really?'

'Yes. But I love you, Jet. More than anything or anyone. Even my mum. You have nothing to worry about as far as me and Garrick are concerned. Things are a bit weird between us and maybe that's what you're seeing or sensing. But I think that's only natural after everything that happened. It doesn't mean I'm going to fall back in love with him, or him with me. It just means we need to work a few things out. You can trust me. I won't do anything to risk losing you. I love you far too much for that.' She stood on tiptoe and kissed him briefly on the lips.

'I do trust you. As I said before, it's Garrick that concerns me.'

'It takes two to tango.' She kissed his chin.

'True.' He grinned at her. 'Do you fancy getting home and doing a bit of tangoing? Is that a word? I don't even care.' He bent his head and kissed her.

'I'll race you,' Mia said, easing herself away from him as she turned to run down Lily Pond Lane.

'Er, Mia.' He jingled his car keys in the air. 'I brought my car, remember. But you're welcome to run home if you like.'

Mia laughed. 'I don't think you're the only one whose brain has turned to mush.' She turned back and arm in arm they walked the metre or so to where his car was parked on the lane.

Chapter Fourteen

Mia was in love with Jet, not Garrick, so she made a decision. No matter what happened, from now on, she would make sure that she and Garrick were never alone unless there was absolutely no alternative. Garrick was a good man, so he probably wouldn't try anything, and she definitely wouldn't be making any moves on him, but even so. Better to be safe than sorry, as Hettie would say. Provided they kept a reasonable distance, and someone else was there, everything would be fine. It was only natural for both of them to harbour some residual feelings for one another, wasn't it? But love? She loved Garrick as a friend and nothing more. And he felt the same way about her, didn't he?

The only reason she needed to be wary was because Garrick clearly wasn't himself at the moment. And who could expect him to be after what he had been through? He had just lost the woman he loved; the mother of his child; the person he thought he would be spending the rest of his life with. The world had been pulled from under him. It was perfectly reasonable and rational that he would try to find something or someone to cling on to at such a time. And completely understandable that the person he would gravitate towards would be Mia; the woman he was hoping to marry only a few months ago.

Once he had settled into life at Sunbeam Cottage and regained his bearings, he would begin to come to terms with his grief and he wouldn't look to the past. Would he? He would try to find a future for himself and Flora, and he must know, deep down, that his future could never be with Mia.

There was a chance that she had misread the signs, and that she had imagined he had feelings for her other than friendship. Just because he'd said he was thinking about her, it didn't mean in a romantic way … even if he had said it was one of the reasons he wasn't sleeping. Perhaps she was seeing things that weren't there. But Jet had seen something in the way Garrick had looked at her, so she couldn't have misjudged the situation entirely.

She had made the right decision. She would simply have to ensure that each time she and Garrick were together, there was at least one other person with them. And not merely baby Flora.

Thanks to Alexia Bywater, Mia didn't even have to try.

'Why is it,' Mia asked Ella, exactly one week after the evening they had babysat, 'that every time I come here lately, Alexia's either coming, going, or firmly ensconced in the kitchen or sitting room?'

Ella shook her head. 'I know. I was asking Gill precisely that myself only yesterday.'

'What did he say?'

'He told me to ask Garrick or Alexia.'

'And have you?'

She nodded. 'Garrick. Who looked at me as if I was a moron and said he had no idea what I was talking about. I pointed out that the woman's been here every day for a week. Sometimes twice a day. He thought about it for a second, shrugged, and said he hadn't been keeping count and he was surprised that I had. He also asked me if I objected to him having friends round to the cottage. Bloody cheek. As if I would! I realise he's grieving, but he knows me better than that.'

'Wow! What did you say?'

Ella cringed. 'I behaved like a complete bitch. I told him that just because someone he loved had died, it didn't mean he needed to turn into a total jerk. Which funnily enough, made him laugh. He said that it was good that he and I were back on our normal footing of loving siblings, slagging one another off in the best possible taste. And he didn't mean that sarcastically. He genuinely is glad that we can be sarcastic, facetious and downright unpleasant to one another, but in a loving, caring, and jokey way.'

Mia laughed and nodded. 'I always loved that about you two. You could say what you felt to one another and neither of you would take the slightest offence. And you could joke and banter together better than anyone else I've ever met.'

'Yeah. It's great to have that back. But it still didn't deal with the Alexia issue. Although even I have to admit, she has actually been pretty helpful. I don't know how or why she knows so much about babies. She says it's from her years of babysitting in the village, but when Flora had a bit of a temperature yesterday afternoon, and Bear was in the middle of an operation on a dog, Alexia, who once again had popped in, calmly took control and handled the situation. By the time Bear arrived, Flora's temperature was back to normal and Bear said he couldn't have handled it any better himself.'

'Really? Beautiful, smart, body of a goddess, top-class rugby player and now first-rate nurse. Are there any limits to Alexia's talents?'

'It appears not. And the worst part was I had to eat crow. Not literally, you understand.'

Mia laughed again. 'I know what 'eating crow' means. You don't have to be a smarty-pants editor to know an expression like that. So Garrick rubbed your face in it, did he?'

'And then some.' Ella shook her head, pulled a face, and grinned. 'He asked if I minded if he put the pub phone number on the landline shortcuts menu. Then, whether or not I was considering apologising. And finally, whether it might not be a bad idea to see if Alexia would like the job of Flora's full-time nanny.'

Mia choked on the wine she was drinking. 'What? I didn't know he was looking for a nanny.'

Ella tutted and gave Mia a playful shove. 'He's not, you idiot. He was being facetious.'

'Are you sure? Having a nanny would actually make sense. It would mean he wouldn't have to rely on any of us being around if he wanted to go somewhere, or do some work. It would also give Flora a routine. Not that she probably has any idea what's going on, but still.'

'I suppose that's true. But I can't see Alexia wanting the position, can you? Besides, don't you have to have some sort of certificate, and be checked out, if you're going to be working with kids? With a prison record, I'm not sure Alexia would be accepted. Not that I know anything about the subject.'

'Neither do I.' Mia sipped her wine, frowning as a thought occurred to her. 'Isn't there any tension, or atmosphere between Garrick and Alexia?'

Ella frowned too. 'No. Why?'

'Because of last year. It wasn't only me, Jet, and her family she was nasty to. She said she only dated Garrick to use him to gain access to the cottage and to find out as much as she could about Mattie's will. Didn't you tell him?'

Ella looked thoughtful. 'No. Well, I didn't think he'd want to hear that he was being used by Alexia and that she didn't care about him at all, even if he only dated her because she looks so much like Fiona and then dumped her to be with you. I did tell him all the things she said about everyone else though. But the first time she came here the other day, she apologised profusely to me. She'd already apologised to Gill before I came home, apparently. In the pub, not here. And she'd also apologised to Garrick this time last week, when they were playing rugby. He said he was a bit surprised because other than those notes she left for you, which he found, he didn't think she had anything to apologise to him for.'

'Because you hadn't told him what she said.'

'Yeah.'

'So Garrick, along with everyone else apart from you and me it seems, truly believes Alexia has put her wicked ways behind her.'

'It seems so.' Ella topped up their wine glasses.

'Jet says I should believe it too.' Mia fiddled with her glass. 'I was moaning about the fact that she's constantly here and he asked me why that was a problem. I said it was because I didn't trust her. Especially around a baby. He laughed. And now I come to think about it, he said that Alexia had a special way with babies. He'd seen it

112

himself. I should've asked how he'd seen it, but it didn't occur to me at the time because he went on to ask whether it was really the baby I was worried about Alexia being around, or whether it was Garrick.'

'Garrick? Does he think you're jealous?'

Mia nodded. 'I think perhaps he does. He asked me why I wasn't prepared to give Alexia the benefit of the doubt. He reminded me that last year, I was constantly telling him how people could change if they wanted to. That's true. I was. I told him I had changed. Fiona had changed her mind about not wanting a baby. Mum had changed by taking a risk on Franklin. And of course, I told Jet he could change from being the man who only believed in having short-term flings with women, to being a man who embraced being in a loving, long-term relationship. He said that for someone who had been so adamant about it, and in his case, persuasive, he couldn't understand why I wasn't prepared to believe that Alexia had changed too.'

Ella tucked her legs beneath her and sighed. 'I suppose, when you look at it like that, we should give her a chance.'

'I suppose so. But I still think a small part of me won't be at all surprised if she does something awful again.'

Chapter Fifteen

'Happy Valentine's Day!'

Mia opened her eyes and blinked. Apart from the bedside lamp, which had momentarily blinded her, the bedroom was shrouded in darkness. The curtains were still closed and not even a chink of twilight was visible.

'What time is it?' She had had another bad night, and yawned as she spoke.

'Time you got up, sleepyhead.' Jet tugged at her foot beneath the duvet. 'Don't you want your present?'

That got her attention. She struggled to sit up. 'Happy Valentine's Day to you! What've you bought me?'

'Give me a kiss first.' He was sitting on the edge of the bed, fully clothed.

'You're dressed?'

'It's seven-thirty. I've been up and dressed since five.'

'Why didn't you wake me sooner?'

'Because you got hardly any sleep again last night and when I woke up, you were actually snoring, so I didn't want to disturb you too soon.'

She gasped. 'You lie! I don't snore.'

He laughed. 'You do. But it's cute.'

'Really?'

'Really.' He kissed her on the lips. 'Now are you getting up?'

She grinned at him. 'It's Valentine's Day. I'd rather you came back to bed.'

He returned the grin. 'So would I. Sadly, I've got a farm to run. But maybe later I could take a break.'

'So where's my present?'

He handed her a large, pink envelope. 'Here's your card. You'll have to come downstairs for your present.'

She eagerly tore open the envelope and pulled out a gorgeous card. It had the words: 'To the One I Love' in embossed silver on the front, together with several silver embossed hearts. It also had a picture of a man holding a large, pink and glitter embossed heart out to a woman who was sitting on a garden swing, surrounded by beautiful flowers and flitting white doves and multicoloured butterflies. Inside the words: 'Be Mine Forever' were printed in silver and surrounded by more pink, glittery hearts. Beneath that, a simple question mark had been added, written with a silver pen, together with the words: 'Not just For Ever. For Eternity and Beyond.'

Mia held the card against her chest with her arms across it, and beamed at Jet. 'This is such a beautiful card. Now where's the one from you?'

He laughed, and prising the card from her, placed it carefully on the floor before gently throwing her back against the pillows.

'You're such a comedienne. I'll make you pay for that.'

He pretended to bite her neck, but it soon turned into kisses and within the space of a few minutes, Mia had thrown his clothes onto the floor to join the card, and Jet seemed to have forgotten that he had work to do.

'That was your present,' she said, twenty minutes later. 'I hope you liked it.'

'Very much, thank you. Now come downstairs and get yours.'

They didn't take their eyes off one another as they dressed; Jet in the clothes Mia had thrown onto the floor, Mia in the jeans and jumper she had worn the day before and tossed onto the back of her dressing table chair last night.

'I'll come back up and have a shower later,' she said. 'You can join me if you want.'

Jet laughed. 'I don't know how I ever manage to get any work done around here.'

Mia laughed too. 'You've got good staff.'

They went downstairs together, hand-in-hand, and Jet led her towards the front door.

'Where are we going?'

He didn't reply. Instead, he opened the front door and stood to one side.

'Ta dah!' He spread his arms and pointed one hand towards a shiny new, red, Volvo XC40, a compact SUV. 'You haven't replaced your car, so I thought I'd do it for you. If you don't like it, that's fine. I know the dealer well and we can exchange it for something else.'

It took a while for Mia to be able to speak. 'Oh my God, Jet! I love it! It's exactly the car I've been looking at. Well, this one and the new Jaguar, but I'd feel like a bit of a show off driving the new Jag around Little Pondale. Thank you *so* much.' She flung her arms around his neck and kissed his face, his neck and his hands. 'I love you to bits.'

'Phew.' He wiped his hand across his brow before smiling at her. 'I knew you wouldn't want jewellery. You've got all of Mattie's and you rarely wear it. Perfume was one of the presents I gave you at Christmas, so I didn't want to get that. But I saw you looking at this online the other day. It's not your only present. We're going out for a romantic dinner tonight, in Little Whitingdale. Some celebrity chef called Xavier something or other has opened a restaurant there with a mate of mine, so I've managed to get us a table.'

'Xavier Sombeanté! You're kidding? He's my idol. Since I've started learning how to cook, he's my go-to guy for recipes.'

Jet laughed. 'Is he?'

Mia stopped jumping up and down with excitement and looked Jet in the eye. 'You know me so well, don't you? I adore you, Jet Cross. Really I do.'

He smiled. 'I merely pay attention.'

'Can I take the car for a drive? Will you come with me?'

'Of course.'

'Oh. But you probably want your present, don't you?'

'Seeing you so happy is all I want, Mia.'

'I believe that. But you're getting your present anyway. Well, you're not actually getting it today, but you'll get to see what it is. Then we're coming straight back here and taking this baby for a ride.' She took his hand in hers and led him into the sitting room. She bent down and pulled a huge card from under the sofa.

'It's bigger than mine,' he said.

'Size doesn't matter, Jet.' She winked at him. 'I've told you that before.'

He grinned. 'Don't get cheeky.'

He opened the card and his surprise at seeing a farmer, standing in the middle of a field with his hands on his hips, adopting a pose like a super-hero, surrounded by a crowd of much smaller men, was evident.

'I had it specially made. You can do that when you're rich.'

The words: 'You're My Hero' were emblazoned across the top and inside it read: You stood out from the crowd the moment I saw you. I want you to stand by my side, for all eternity.'

Jet actually looked as if he had a tear in his eye but he pulled her into his arms so she couldn't see his face.

'God, Mia. I love you so, so much. I never thought it was possible to love anyone as much as I love you. Thank you. This is the best card I've ever had.'

'I'm glad you like it. If you let me breathe, I'll show you your present.'

He released her and quickly swiped at his eyes. 'Dust.'

She nodded. 'Obviously.'

She handed him a car magazine with a sticky note attached to one of the pages. He flicked straight to it and his eyes opened wide and so did his mouth.

'This? You've got me this?'

'I've never seen anyone get so excited about a magazine before.'

'Actually, I'd be perfectly happy with the magazine.'

'I know you would. That's another reason I adore you. But no. The only reason you don't have the real thing is because it isn't in stock yet. But it is on order.'

'It's out in April. Are you serious? This is a pricey SUV, Mia.'

She shrugged. 'BMWs don't come cheap. But you're worth every penny. I know you don't need a new car because you only replaced yours last October, but I heard you and Gill the other day, talking about how great the new BMW X7 looks, so I pulled him to one side when you were making coffee and asked him to help me.'

'Oh, so that's why he asked me what colour I'd choose. I assume that means I'll be getting the Arctic Grey Metallic?'

He looked like he'd been given the world on a platter. But she couldn't help but tease him. 'Oh I thought Gill said the white one. Sorry.'

He smiled. 'That's okay. The colour doesn't matter. It's wonderful, Mia. You're wonderful.'

'And you're getting the grey one, you wonderful dope.'

He lifted her in his arms and swung her round and round.

'This is the best Valentine's ever.'

'It is. But you'd better put me down or I'll be too dizzy to drive my new car.'

Chapter Sixteen

Mia loved her new car. After she and Jet had driven it through Little Pondale, waving and smiling at everyone they passed, she dropped Jet back at the farm.

'I must do some work today,' he joked. 'Or people will start to talk.'

'And I must take a shower and get to Ella's. She's cooking Gill a surprise five-course dinner and I promised to help. So did Mum. And let's be honest, Mum will end up doing most of it, but it's the thought that counts. I can't wait to show them my car.'

'Don't forget our table's booked for eight. We'll need to leave by seven fifteen to be on the safe side.'

'I'll be home by five.'

'Make it four-thirty. I know what you're like.' He kissed her, grinned and marched down the side of the farmhouse to the yard, waving and shouting: 'I love you. Missing you already.'

It took Mia less than twenty minutes to shower, dress and get back in her car. She would have breakfast at Ella's. It had completely slipped her mind that she hadn't eaten until her stomach rumbled as she put on her boots.

She sped down the lane and was parking at Sunbeam Cottage just as Alexia was coming out.

'Happy Valentine's Day,' Alexia said. 'Nice wheels.'

'Thanks. Jet bought them for me for Valentine's. We're going out to dinner this evening too, at a brand-new restaurant owned by one of Jet's friends and the famous chef, Xavier Sombeanté.'

'Oh, Luke Martindale's new place? I've heard that's fantastic. We went to school with him. And Xavier Sombeanté is fabulous. I watch his TV show all the time.'

Alexia knew the co-owner? Well, that served Mia right for showing off, didn't it?

'Me too. What are you up to tonight?'

'It seems Garrick and I are the only two single people in Little Pondale, so we're having dinner together in the pub. Ella's got something planned for Gill, and Garrick doesn't want to be in the way.'

At least Alexia had the decency to look embarrassed. Mia was tempted to remind her that she'd said only last October that she had no interest in Garrick whatsoever, but that would be mean, and Mia had promised Jet to try to give Alexia a chance.

'That sounds like a good idea. Who's looking after Flora?'

'We're taking her with us. Dad's going to keep an eye on her while we're eating. We'll join them in the sitting room afterwards, till Garrick thinks he can sneak back here without barging in on Ella and Gill. I'd better go. I promised Toby I'd do the lunchtime shift because he and Christy are working this evening. Bye. Have a wonderful night.'

'You too.'

Mia watched her for a second or two before running to the door of Sunbeam Cottage.

'Perhaps Alexia has changed after all,' she said, when Ella opened it.

'Why? Oh. She told you about tonight, did she?' They stood at the door and watched as Alexia walked up Lily Pond Lane. 'I told Garrick he was welcome to join us but he wouldn't hear of it. When Alexia came round this morning and suggested it, I was almost grateful.'

'It was Alexia who suggested it?'

'Yeah. You didn't think Garrick would ask her out, did you?'

'But it's not a date, is it?'

Ella smirked. 'They both say it isn't but I'm not so sure. The two of them are thicker than thieves these days. But he does still spend a lot of time staring at photos of Fiona, and once or twice, I've heard him crying, so I don't think he's ready to date anyone yet. Sex, of course, is an entirely different matter. They're both single so if that's where this leads, and they're both okay with it, I suppose he could do worse. Wait a minute.' Ella peered over Mia's shoulder. 'Is that a new car?'

Mia nodded with excitement. 'Jet's Valentine present to me. Well, one of them. We're going to Xavier Sombeanté's new restaurant for dinner.'

'Wow! He's really pushing the boat out. Let me come and look at it. Gill got me this.' She waggled the delicate silver bracelet on her wrist.

'That's gorgeous, Ella.' They walked to Mia's car and Ella got in the passenger seat. 'Does he know about the dinner yet?'

'Swanky.' Ella pushed various buttons and reclined the seat 'Yep. I gave him a handmade invitation in his card. At first he thought it was a joke. Until I hit him.' She tutted and raised her brows as she sat upright. 'I didn't really hit him, but I was tempted. He'll have to apologise profusely tonight. Of course I won't be telling him that Lori cooked most of it. She is coming, isn't she? Franklin hasn't whisked her off somewhere on a white horse, his Stetson in one hand, the reins in the other?'

Mia laughed at that image. 'Not as far as I know. I called to tell her about my present and she said she'd be here around noon.'

'Great. Let's get started. I love this car. Can I borrow it sometime?'

'Why don't I buy you one of your own for your birthday? Or it could be a late Christmas present. I don't know why I didn't buy you one before now.'

Ella shoved the door open and laughed. 'Thanks. But I don't need one. Gill drives me anywhere I want to go.'

'Well, if you change your mind, just say the word. And yes, you can borrow this one if you like.'

'That's a deal. And if I'm not mistaken, here comes Lori. This is going to be a fantastic day. I feel it in my water.'

'Ew. Thanks for sharing.'

Linking arms, they waited for Lori to park and when she'd also given Mia's car the once over, they walked to the cottage and into the kitchen where Garrick was seated at the table, Flora in his arms, giving her her bottle.

'Happy Valentine's Day,' Mia said. Why did her stomach do that every time she saw Garrick holding Flora? A sort of tumble. Not wholly unpleasant but extremely disconcerting.

He glanced up and smiled. 'And to you. And you, Lori. Get anything nice?'

'A car, and dinner tonight,' Mia said.

Lori smiled. 'Sexy underwear, gorgeous flowers and a weekend in Paris in the Spring.'

'Wow!' said Ella. Mia already knew.

'That's impressive,' Garrick said.

'I hear you're going out with Alexia.' Mia hadn't meant to mention it. It slipped out.

'It's not a date.' He gave her an odd look.

'I know. It'll be good for you. To get out, I mean. With a woman. I'll shut up now.'

'Please do,' Ella said, shoving her towards the counter. 'We need to peel some onions. Up for that?'

'Do I have a choice?'

'No.' Ella handed Mia a knife and took one for herself. 'We'll follow your instructions, Lori.'

Garrick got to his feet. 'I think we'd better get out of here. My sister with sharp pointy things near a baby is not a good idea.' He laughed as he left the room with Flora still cradled in his arms.

Didn't that baby ever cry? Mia hadn't heard her make a sound, unless a gurgle counted. She did fart quite a bit though. And for someone so tiny, boy did they pong.

'Right,' Lori said, looking at Ella. 'We'll start with the dessert because that's the hardest part. Have you ever made a Pavlova?'

'No.'

'A meringue of any sort?'

'No.'

'Oh dear. This may take longer than I thought. Let's get cracking. And I mean that literally. We need eggs, girls. Lots of eggs.'

'I brought those,' Mia said, removing a container with more than a dozen eggs from her shoulder bag and placing it on the counter. 'Freshly laid this morning, courtesy of our Little Pond Farm chickens.'

'Did you wash them?' Ella removed the lid and grabbed a sheet of paper kitchen towel, picking a lump of what resembled chicken poo from one of them.

'Just wipe them with some of that towel,' Lori said, a little wearily, considering she'd only just arrived. 'We're not using the shells.' She raised her eyes skywards and shook her head.

The plan was to make a Pavlova and add a heart-shaped 'lake' in the middle made of fondant icing with blue food colouring, and two swans to 'float' on top. A nod to the fact that Gill had taken her to see Swan Lake, and that her surname was Swann. The Pavlova would have two layers and in the centre there'd be cream, pears, pecan nuts and lots of butterscotch sauce, all of which were Gill's favourites.

'At least the starter's easy, isn't it?' Mia said. 'I can help make that. Smoked salmon wrapped around asparagus, with Hollandaise sauce. But you'll have to make the softly boiled egg, just before you serve it.'

'Who's making the Hollandaise sauce?' Lori asked.

Mia and Ella exchanged confused looks.

'Making it?' Ella queried. 'It comes in a jar. I bought two.'

Lori sighed, and shook her head again.

It took them several hours to do everything, and even with Garrick coming to help, by the time all five courses were ready, it was four-forty-five and they were all covered in a mixture of flour, sugar, butterscotch sauce, potato peel and a lot more besides. There was even a slice of onion in Mia's hair, which Garrick kindly removed.

'I've got to go. I promised Jet I'd be home fifteen minutes ago.' Mia hurried to the door. 'Good luck, Ella. I hope it all goes well. Bye Mum. Bye Garrick.'

She was at the car before she realised she hadn't got her bag or her keys. She raced back up the drive, meeting Garrick on his way down.

'I forgot my…' She didn't need to finish the sentence. Garrick held her bag in one hand, her keys in the other. 'Thanks. I'd forget my head if it wasn't screwed on.' She smiled at him and turned back towards the car.

'Mia?'

'Yes.'

He was right behind her. He reached out and removed another piece of onion, this time from her cheek. 'You seem to be wearing most of Ella's dinner.'

'Let's hope Gill isn't later,' she joked. Ella had threatened to throw it over his head if he didn't like it after all the work they'd put in.

'She did say she'd be covering him in butterscotch sauce in any event.' He gave her an odd look and a quirky little smile. 'Do you remember when I did that to you with melted chocolate and licked it off?'

She coughed lightly. 'Yes. Of course.'

'I miss us, Mia. I know I shouldn't, but I do.'

'Garrick. Please. You miss Fiona, not me. You miss the company. The feeling of togetherness. Of being part of a couple. It's completely understandable. But you don't really miss me.'

'You're wrong. I miss you. I miss this. I still feel so guilty about Fiona and I loved her. You know I did. I still do. But I loved you just as much. And I'm not sure I'll ever stop loving you.'

She shook her head. 'No. You don't. You will stop. It's just today. Days like this make us all crazy. There's so much pressure to love and be loved on Valentine's Day. I love Jet, Garrick. I'm sorry. I really am. But I can't have this conversation. I can't. I care about you as a friend. A dear friend, but that's all it can ever be now. All it will ever be. I don't want to hurt you, but I'm sure, once you're more yourself, you'll regret saying this.'

He sighed deeply and looked her in the eye. 'Perhaps you're right. God, I'm sorry. I don't know what I'm doing anymore.'

She shouldn't have done it, but she wasn't thinking clearly. He looked so sad, hurt, broken and lonely. She leant forward, stood on her tiptoes and kissed him on the cheek.

She meant it to be a quick peck; nothing more, but before she knew it, his arms were around her in a tight embrace and his mouth was on hers.

It lasted for a matter of seconds. Two or three at the most, but when she pushed him away and saw the longing in his eyes she knew it was a dreadful mistake.

'That shouldn't have happened, Garrick. And it never will again. I think it's best if I stay away for a while. Give you time to sort yourself out. I want us to be friends. I'm sorry. I've got to go.'

She turned and ran down the drive, got in her car and didn't look back as she sped away. It was only as she pulled up outside the farmhouse, spotted Jet in the near distance and watched him leading the reindeer back to the barn that a terrible thought struck her.

What if someone had seen them?

Would that person or persons have realised that Garrick kissed her; she didn't kiss him? Other than the peck on his cheek, that is.

That she'd pushed him away immediately. Well, almost immediately. It had taken a second or two to realise what was happening.

She shook her head and dismissed the notion.

No one had seen them. She was worrying about nothing. She should forget it happened and go and make herself look as good as she could for Jet tonight. Dismiss it from her mind and never think of it or speak of it again.

She must definitely stay away from Garrick for the next few days at least. He couldn't possibly have meant the things he'd said. He'd simply been swept up by the fun they'd had that afternoon and because it was Valentine's Day, he was understandably feeling uber-emotional. He'd regret that kiss tomorrow.

Jet waved at her as he neared the gate that led behind the house and garden to the yard. He tapped his watch with his finger and she could see that he was laughing, but she couldn't hear what he said. She waved back, climbed out of the car and ran into the house. The sooner she got into the shower the better. It was ridiculous, but as she breathed in, all she could smell was the subtle scent of Garrick's aftershave.

Chapter Seventeen

The last person Mia expected to hear from the following morning was Garrick.

Her evening with Jet had been wonderful – apart from not being able to rid herself of the ridiculous feeling of guilt over that kiss from Garrick.

Some of the many highlights had been the two dozen red roses that were waiting for her in the vase on her dressing table, the champagne on ice, the limo to take them to the restaurant and back, and Jet giving her yet another present at their table at the restaurant. It was Xavier Sombeanté's new recipe book.

But the icing on her Valentine's cake had been meeting the man himself. Jet's friend, Luke Martindale, co-owner of the restaurant had introduced them. And the cherry on the top had been when Xavier had signed his book with a personal and friendly message to Mia and invited her to come back one day for a private lesson. He'd even said she could bring a friend or two if she liked. And not in a suggestive way, as Ella would've said if she'd been there.

'This has been the best day of my life,' she told Jet as they lay in bed later, after an hour or so of making love and long, tender kisses.

'And mine. Equal only to Christmas morning when you said yes after I proposed.'

'Oh yes. Same here,' she said, snuggling closer. 'We haven't set a date yet.'

'No. And we should. I'm seeing Glen tomorrow morning. Shall I mention it to him and ask him to let us know when he's got a free date in his diary? Or would you rather do that?'

'No. I'm happy for you to do it. Although please run it by me before agreeing to one. I know quite a lot of our friends already have plans for this year and I'd like them all to be there, wouldn't you? Oh.' She glanced up at him. 'That is, if you mean this year. Next year is fine. Or whenever you want.'

Jet laughed and kissed her nose. 'The sooner the better as far as I'm concerned. I'd like you to be my wife before anyone else has a chance to steal you away.'

'That will never happen. Ever. You're stuck with me for life, mister.' She hugged him tighter to prove her point.

Or was it because that niggling feeling of guilt still wouldn't leave her in peace?

So Garrick really was the last person she wanted to hear from, and when she saw Ella's name on the caller display while eating toast in the kitchen, around ten, she answered immediately.

'How did your night go? Did Gill enjoy his dinner, or is he still wearing it this morning?'

'What? Oh. It's Garrick, Mia. Please don't hang up. Is Jet there? You and I need to talk.'

She gasped in surprise. 'No, he isn't. And no, we don't. There's nothing to talk about. It was a mistake Garrick and we should both forget it happened.'

'I agree it was a mistake, in the cold light of day. But sadly, neither of us can forget it happened and for that, I'm truly sorry. Alexia saw us, Mia. She was coming out of Jenny's and was on her way to Hettie's. She asked me last night why I was kissing you on the drive of Sunbeam Cottage.'

Chapter Eighteen

When Garrick had said those fateful words, Mia was sure she'd been sucked off the earth by a black hole and was tumbling around in an unknown universe where everything was dark and cold and lonely.

He'd said that he told Alexia it meant nothing. That it was he who kissed Mia, not the other way around, and that Mia was really angry with him for doing it. He had virtually pleaded with Alexia to keep it to herself and had actually begged her not to tell Jet.

'Why would I do that?' Alexia had said. 'These things happen. It shouldn't ruin people's lives.'

'Does that mean she will or won't be keeping it to herself?' Mia asked.

'I think it means she will. In fact, I'm pretty sure it does. But I thought I should warn you, just in case. People can be so unpredictable.'

'Tell me about it. God, Garrick, if Jet finds out, he'll be furious. And not just furious, but devastated. It took ages for me to break through the barriers he'd put up to stop himself from getting hurt, and now this happens. He'll be heartbroken.'

'It was just a kiss, Mia. And not even a proper kiss. It only lasted for a few seconds.'

'It shouldn't have happened at all. Are you telling me that you would brush it aside if you found out that the one person you loved deeply had kissed someone else? Even for one second, let alone a few.'

Garrick had taken a moment to reply. 'No. I probably wouldn't. I'd feel hurt and betrayed and it would take me a while to trust that person again.'

'Bloody hell, Garrick. You see! Now times that feeling by about ten and you'll have some idea of how Jet will take it. Thanks very much for ruining my day.'

'I'm sorry, Mia. Really I am. What more can I say? Do you want me to talk to Jet about it?'

'What? No, I bloody well don't. We'll just have to hope and pray that Alexia really is a changed woman and that she has the decency to see it for what it was and keep the whole damn thing to herself. Goodbye.'

She'd slammed the phone down and screamed her head off, so much so that Pete, who was working in the yard, heard it and came rushing into the kitchen. Thank Goodness Jet was at Glen's.

'Mia? You okay, love? What's happened?'

'Oh God, Pete. You startled me. Um. Nothing's happened. I … I just thought I saw a mouse. But I was wrong.'

'A mouse?' He didn't look convinced. 'Well, if you see it again, come and get me or Franklin. Try not to scream the place down, love. I thought you were dying for a minute there, and Jet would've killed me if you were. This old heart doesn't need that sort of shock.'

'I'm so sorry, Pete. I promise I won't do it again.'

'Okay then.' He gave her another odd look and finally closed the door behind him, saying: 'A mouse. It's probably had a heart attack. Poor little bugger.'

When she was certain he was out of earshot, she grabbed a kitchen chair and banged it up and down against the tiled floor, gritting her teeth and making a Grrrr-like sound for at least five seconds. Thankfully, the chair was made of sturdy stuff and didn't break because how she would've explained that to Jet she had no idea. Especially if Pete told him about the supposed mouse.

Not long after she'd managed to calm herself down, Jet returned from the village. He had a strange look on his face when he entered the kitchen, a cake box from Lake's Bakes in one hand, a loaf of heavenly-smelling, freshly baked bread under his arm. He didn't look angry exactly, more like confused.

Mia tried to remain calm, and switched on the kettle but she was preparing herself for the worst as she walked back towards the table.

'I've just seen Alexia. She was going into Jenny's as I was leaving and she told me some extraordinary news. I assume you know, but I'm surprised you haven't told me.'

He was far too calm and controlled. Perhaps he was in shock.

'Oh God, Jet' she said, gripping the back of the slightly battered chair. 'I was going to, but I didn't want to make it seem as if it was important. Because it isn't.'

He frowned, a perplexed look in his eyes. 'I think it is. And to be honest, I'm surprised you don't.'

'It meant nothing, Jet.' She dashed to him and grabbed the sleeve of his jacket. 'Please believe me. It lasted for a matter of seconds. I knew that bitch would blab. I knew she hadn't changed.'

An anxious look crept across his face and fear filled his eyes and this time when he spoke, there was a distinct edge to his voice.

'What lasted for a matter of seconds?'

Oh God! He didn't know. Or was this his way of seeing if she would tell him the truth?

'What, Mia? Tell me.' The edge was sharper.

Tentatively, reluctantly she whispered: 'The kiss.'

He sucked in a breath as if he were gasping for air. 'What kiss?'

'It was nothing, Jet. A stupid mistake. A misunderstanding. Honestly. I love you.'

'What kiss, Mia? Or should I go and ask Garrick? I suppose I can safely assume he was involved?' The edge cut like a knife.

She tried to swallow but the lump in her throat wouldn't budge. Even to her ears, her voice sounded like she was chewing gravel.

'I didn't know what was happening. I forgot my bag and keys. He ran after me. Brought them. We'd had a lovely afternoon. He didn't mean what he said. He looked so sad. So lonely. I meant it as a friendly peck. Nothing more. He kissed me. But honestly just for a couple of seconds. I pushed him away. Alexia saw us. She said she wouldn't tell you, but she did. I knew she would.'

Slowly, oh so slowly he took her hand in his – and flung it away from him as if it scalded him, and stepped back with a look on his face that indicated he couldn't bear to be near her.

'I assume that means you had no intention of telling me yourself? If it was such a harmless, meaningless kiss, why wouldn't you do that?' His voice and his eyes were cold.

What could she say? That she hadn't told him because she knew this was how he would react? That she knew he would be devastated. That would go down like a dead cow falling on his head.

She gave a pitiful shrug and a pleading look and for a split second, he seemed to waver.

He took one step towards her, and then he clenched his fists, locked his jaw and set his kissable lips in a scowl. His eyes were like ice when he turned to walk away, but he stopped and glowered at her. 'For your information, Alexia didn't breathe a word.'

'But … you said she gave you news?' Mia's heart was breaking but she had to understand how this had all gone so horribly wrong.

He snorted in derision, his voice bitter now, but cracking with emotion, his eyes hard, his fists still clenched. 'She did. Although now, it's even more surprising. She told me that she thought she was falling in love with Garrick and that she hoped, given time, he might feel the same about her. If she saw you two kissing as you say she did, I'm surprised she's so eager to forgive him.' He turned away again and back. 'She has changed, Mia, even though you're determined not to believe it. Now I see why. And she's not a bitch. I think that's the pot calling the kettle black, isn't it?'

This time he did walk away. Stormed away to be precise, and Little M, who had been curled up in her basket, pricked up her ears, gave one short, sharp growl and scampered after her master, reaching his side moments before he slammed the kitchen door behind them.

Despite desperately wanting to race after him to beg for his forgiveness, Mia's legs wouldn't move. Had Jet just called her a bitch? A bitch? If not for the chair, she would've crumpled into a heap on the floor.

How could a day begin on such a high, and end on such a low?

Chapter Nineteen

'I don't know w-what to do!' Mia sobbed on Lori's shoulder, while Ella squeezed Mia's hand and squashed in closer to her on the sofa in the sitting room of Sunbeam Cottage.

'It'll be fine, sweetheart. You'll see.' Lori gently stroked Mia's hair and rocked her in her arms. 'He's cross, that's all. Which is understandable given the circumstances.'

'He's simply living up to his name,' Ella said. 'Jet *Cross*, get it? Oh. Too soon for jokes then?'

'Far too soon,' Lori said, as Mia sobbed louder after giving Ella a look containing at least a thousand daggers.

'But he adores you,' Ella added. 'He'll calm down and give you a chance to explain. Although he may come and punch Garrick in the face first. Which my brother would heartily deserve, quite frankly. I know he's grieving and everything but there are limits.'

'Oh God,' Mia groaned. 'He w-won't, will he? The worst p-part is, he was so c-calm and controlled. But he h-hates me. I c-could see it in his eyes.'

'Pah!' Ella said. 'He doesn't hate you. That man would walk over burning coals for you. He'd fight monsters for you. He'd die for you.' She burst into one of her favourite, Bon Jovi songs, aptly entitled, *I'd Die for You*.

'Ella!' Lori snapped. 'Make yourself useful and go and get Mia a glass of brandy. A large glass.'

'I'm just trying to cheer her up,' Ella protested, but without taking offence. 'This can't be serious, can it? Jet adores you, Mia. It'll all blow over. Won't it?' She glanced at Mia and without another word, dashed to the kitchen, returning to the sitting room cradling three glasses. She grabbed the brandy bottle from the cocktail cabinet and placed it on the coffee table. 'I thought we could all do with one. And there's another bottle in the cabinet if one isn't enough. This one's only half full anyway.'

Mia grabbed the bottle, unscrewed the top and tossed it one the table where it rolled onto the floor. Ignoring that, she took three large gulps of brandy. Ella raised her eyebrows as Mia wiped her mouth with the back of her hand and thumped the bottle back onto the table.

'I'll get another,' Ella said, heading back over to the cocktail cabinet.

'What if one of us has a word with him?' Lori asked.

'Not Garrick,' Ella said, somewhat unhelpfully.

'I was thinking more of Gill.' Lori kissed Mia on her cheek. 'Gill's sensible. Intelligent too. And as a man he'll know exactly what to say in a situation like this.'

Ella pulled a face. 'Gill's got a bit of a hangover. He's gone for a long walk to clear his head. I'm not sure when he'll be back.'

'Well, I'll ask Franklin then. He knows Jet well. He'll know what to do. Or possibly Glen. A vicar is used to this sort of thing, isn't he?' Lori was clearly clutching at straws.

'It's no good, Mum.' Mia grabbed another tissue from the box on her lap and blew her nose with vigour. 'He hates me. It's over. I'll have to move back here. Can I, Ella?'

'Of course you can. It's your cottage anyway. Gill and I will move into his room so you can have your old room back. But I don't think it'll come to that. You won't break up because of one stupid little kiss. Jet's not a jerk. He was once, admittedly, but he's over that phase of his life.'

'It definitely won't come to that.' Lori was emphatic. 'The man's not an idiot. And he won't stop loving you just because you made a silly mistake. It wasn't even your fault. It was Garrick's. Jet will see that and he'll be apologising to you, and begging for your forgiveness. Not the other way around.'

'He won't. He's stubborn. He may have changed, but I'm not sure he'll forgive this. He feels betrayed. His dad broke his mum's heart, remember. Now I've just broken his.'

'I think that's a bit dramatic, darling. A kiss is nothing these days. People kiss each other all the time. Now if you'd slept with Garrick, that's a different matter entirely, but a kiss. Pah. That's just an extension of a smile between two people's lips. If he's prepared to throw away his future with you over something as trivial as that, God alone knows what he'd do if there was a real drama. You did say he was calm and controlled. Perhaps he simply needs to let his anger and frustration out and he'll be as right as rain.'

'At least we know one good thing,' Ella said. 'If what Jet said is true, Alexia really has changed. She could've easily told Jet, but she didn't. I'm not sure about her and Garrick though. The thought of having her for a sister-in-law fills me with trepidation.'

Mia blew her nose again. 'Then I'll be the one who's all alone. I'll be like great-aunt Mattie. Single for the rest of my life, never getting over the man I loved and lost. And years from now, I'll have a heart attack and die and I'll be found lying at the foot of the attic room stairs, just like her.'

'Nonsense,' Ella and Lori said, simultaneously.

'You and Jet will die arm in arm, in bed, probably, with your false teeth in matching jars on the bedside cabinet,' Ella added. 'And Jet will have a separate jar with Garrick's real teeth in it, as a trophy, after he knocks them out.'

Mia chuckled at last. 'God, what a mess. One minute everything's going so well and the next, this happens. The irony is, Jet was going to talk to Glen this morning about seeing if he has a date free for our wedding. I wonder if he did that. If so, that's the second wedding of mine that'll have to be cancelled. No doubt Hettie will have something to say about that.' She burst into tears once more.

She didn't have long to wait to hear what Hettie had to say. As usual the village drums had been beating non-stop.

Hettie knocked on the door of Sunbeam Cottage and burst in without waiting to be invited.

'Is it true? Oh, deary, you're here. And Ella's got the brandy out I see. Any chance of a small glass for me?'

Ella raised her brows, got Hettie a glass from the kitchen, and topped up Mia's now that she had refrained from drinking from the bottle.

'Who told you?' Mia demanded.

Hettie dropped into an armchair near the sofa and Ella squeezed between Hettie's legs and the coffee table to resume her seat.

'Young Garrick. I saw him less than five minutes ago, deary, pushing that little angel of his in the pram. He looked like he'd been run over by

146

the lorry that killed Fiona. I asked him what was wrong and at first he wouldn't tell me, but I got it out of him. What a pickle. That young man needs to set himself some boundaries. I know he's your brother, deary.' She tapped Ella on the knee. 'But goodness me. You can't go around kissing people willy-nilly. And I know dear Jet. That lad won't take this lightly. He'll be as mad as a box of frogs.'

'He is. It's over.' Mia tried to stop herself from crying again, but failed.

'Over?' Hettie said. 'Stuff and nonsense. All that lad needs, deary, is time to vent his spleen. I've known him since he was running around in nappies causing havoc to all and sundry. Believe me, he gave his heart and soul to you and he doesn't want them back.'

'But that's why he's so hurt. Why he feels so betrayed.'

'Yes. But it doesn't mean he's stopped loving you, deary. Give him a bit of time and some space and he'll see sense.'

'She wants to come back here,' Ella said.

'Is that wise?' Hettie glanced at Lori. 'To move in here. The scene of the crime, so to speak. And why move out of Little Pond Farm anyway? It's your home now, deary. It's not a good idea to let an argument fester. Better to have it out and be done with it. I meant, give him time and space at the farm.'

'I don't think I've got much choice. It's his home. If he wants me to leave, I'll have to.'

'It might do him good to spend a day or two without you,' Ella said. 'And the nights. He'll soon realise what he risks losing when he's alone in that big bed of his again. I don't just mean the sex. I mean the companionship, the cuddles, having someone he loves beside him to wake up to. An empty pillow might make him face reality.'

'Or he might go back to his old ways and soon realise he doesn't miss me at all.'

'Now you're really being ridiculous.'

'Yes,' said Lori, agreeing with Ella. 'He loves you far too much for that. And you love him far too much to let him.'

Chapter Twenty

It took Mia a while to decide what to do for the best. If they had had a simple row, she wouldn't have considered moving out of Little Pond Farm, even just for a night or two. But this wasn't a simple row. Jet thought she had betrayed him. Cheated on him with the man she was going to marry before she dated him. While she hoped and prayed they could get over this, she also knew how badly Jet had taken it. And she understood. If the roles had been reversed and Jet had kissed Alexia or someone like that, Mia would've taken it equally as hard.

But she would've forgiven him, once she'd been able to deal with the pain it would've caused her. She had to believe that Jet would do the same. And deep down, she did. But she didn't have Jet's history with his mum and dad. That made the whole thing ten times worse from Jet's point of view. It wasn't a simple kiss, to him. It was a complete betrayal.

She would do what Ella suggested. Not move out; simply give him a day or two to think things through. If he still loved her, she would go running back the minute he clicked his fingers.

'You're leaving?'

Jet stood in the doorway of the kitchen leading out into the hall as Mia came downstairs with her holdall in her hand. Lori was waiting outside in her car, Mia having had far too many brandies to drive. She hadn't seen him there and his voice made her jump, more so because it contained an odd combination of both fear and derision.

'No. Not exactly. I thought you needed some time to think about things, that's all.'

'To think about you and Garrick kissing, you mean? I've thought of nothing else since you told me.'

She sighed wearily. 'I don't want to fight with you, Jet. I love you. I'm sorry. I don't know what else I can say or do to prove it. If I could turn back the clock, I would, but I can't. It's up to you. You must decide if you can forgive me. If we can get over this and move on with our lives.'

He stared at her as if he didn't know what to do. How to react. He leant against the door frame and bowed his head, shaking it slowly.

'It feels as if you've stuck a knife in my heart. I know that sounds dramatic and clichéd, but I can't help it. I was worried about him coming back. I knew something like this might happen.'

'What? So you didn't trust me?'

He raised angry eyes to hers. 'It seems I had good reason not to.'

She was angry now. And also a little drunk. 'I'm sorry, Jet. But I don't think I did anything wrong. I know it seems as if I cheated on you but I didn't. I made a stupid misjudgement, that's all. And it led to something else. But it wasn't something I wanted to happen. I didn't plan to kiss him. I didn't want to kiss him. The only person I want to kiss is you. Ella said I could stay at Sunbeam Cottage–'

'Perfect!' He almost spat the word at her. 'What better way to make me believe that you don't want to be in the arms of your ex than to run straight back to the place where you two lived and slept together. The place where he's living now. Yeah. That'll totally convince me there's nothing going on between the two of you.'

That made her furious. 'There *is* nothing going on. And if you'd let me finish, instead of jumping to completely the wrong conclusions, you'd have heard me say that I didn't want to stay there, so I asked Cathy and Christy if I can stay with them in Corner Cottage for a day or two instead. Leo's in London so it'll just be us girls. Not a man in sight for you to think I may be kissing. You know where I am if you want me. Or if you actually want to listen to what really happened.'

She walked towards the door, her palms sweating, her heart racing, her breath shallow as she tried to stop her legs from buckling beneath her. Going to Corner Cottage had seemed the best plan. She didn't want to stay at her mum's because their cottage was on Jet's farm, and that would be too close for comfort. Hettie's was an option, but Mia couldn't face that. And as much as she dreaded leaving Jet alone at the farmhouse with nothing but his thoughts – and Little M, she couldn't bear to see the look of disdain in his eyes. To be close to him but unable to find comfort in his arms. To see the scowl on those lips in place of the devilish grin she loved so much. To hear the evident hurt in his voice instead of the love and laughter that had been there just a few short hours before.

'Mia?' Jet's voice was cold and hard with the slightest tremor as he glared at her. 'Did you or didn't you kiss Garrick?'

She met his eyes. 'Not in the way you think I did, no. I kissed him on the cheek. The rest was all him. But you're not going to believe that, are you?'

He stared at her but didn't say a word.

'I thought not.'

She opened the door, turned round once to look at him, but he hadn't moved. He did seem to be swaying, slightly. Perhaps he'd hit the brandy bottle too. She took a deep breath and left, closing the door softly behind her.

Would he come after her?

Her hands were shaking as she threw her holdall on the back seat of Lori's car, and she tumbled into the passenger seat, glancing longingly at the front door of the farmhouse, but it remained firmly shut.

'Drive, Mum. Please get me away from here as fast as possible.'

She had hardly finished the sentence before she burst into a flood of tears.

Chapter Twenty-One

'Thanks for this,' Mia said to Cathy and Christy when Lori dropped her off, half an hour later. Mia had needed a good cry after seeing Jet and didn't want to turn up at Corner Cottage blubbing her eyes out. She'd sat in her mum's car, parked at the entrance to Lily Pond Lane, while Lori hugged her. Only once she was sure she had no more tears to weep, did they drive the few metres to her destination.

'It's the least we can do,' said Cathy, with a sympathetic smile.

'I can't believe this is happening,' Christy said. 'You and Jet were the perfect couple.'

'Are the perfect couple,' Cathy corrected. 'This is a tiny hiccup. Nothing more. You'll be back together in no time.'

'I wish I had your confidence.' Mia bit her lip so that she wouldn't cry again.

Cathy reached out and touched Mia's arm. 'Come in. We gave the kids their supper early and they're tucked up in bed, so we can have a good old chinwag, as Hettie might say. We've made some nibbles for us to have with a bottle or two of wine. I don't know about you, but I never feel like eating a proper meal at times like this, and yet give me a barrel of crisps and a bucket of ice cream and I'll scoff those in seconds.'

Cathy took Mia's holdall and Christy took her coat. She followed them into the sitting room and saw several plates and bowls of delicious looking snacks on the coffee table. She had no appetite but Cathy was right, she might have a crisp or two a bit later. And perhaps, some ice cream.

'I've got to work in the pub tonight,' Christy told her, flopping into an armchair. 'So it'll just be you and Cathy for most of the evening.'

Cathy nodded and ushered Mia towards the sofa. 'But don't feel under any pressure to stay up. If you want to go to bed, or lounge in a bath for hours, please just say so. Treat this as your own home. Don't stand on ceremony with us.'

Mia was grateful for their understanding, but she could use the company. She perched on the edge of the sofa, suddenly feeling rather awkward. She'd only known them since they arrived at Christmas and although they had become friends, it wasn't the same as being with Ella. But then she had known Ella all her life. Ella and Garrick.

No. She didn't want to think about Garrick tonight.

Christy grabbed a stick with chunks of chicken on and dipped the meat in what looked like Satay sauce. Before taking a bite she said: 'I don't understand what happened. If you'd rather not say, that's fine.'

Mia shook her head. 'I'm not absolutely certain myself. It was all just a silly misunderstanding, but it's blown out of all proportion. Not only does Jet think I've betrayed him. He also thinks I tried to hide it from him.'

She told them the story, in between sips of wine, and when she'd finished, she grabbed a handful of crisps and finally sat back in the sofa, feeling a little more relaxed in their company but teetering on the edge of tears once again.

They looked at one another and Christy asked: 'Why is Jet so worked up over a stupid little kiss, anyway?'

Mia munched the crisps before disclosing a bit about Jet's mum and dad. She didn't want to divulge everything because that was Jet's story to tell, not hers, but she told them enough to make them understand why Jet would see a simple thing like a kiss, as the tip of the iceberg. She also explained that she and Garrick had history. She told them all about last year.

'Ah,' Cathy said. 'We'd heard some of it of course and you told us snippets, I remember, but it hadn't twigged that Garrick was that guy, for some reason.'

Christy nodded. 'What with all the excitement between Hettie and Leo over Leo's real dad, the Christmas celebrations, both of us falling in love and everything else that happened over Christmas and New Year, I'm not sure either of us took in half of the stories we were told. For such a small village, there does seem to be an awful lot of drama and excitement. And now Alexia's back, we wouldn't be surprised if there's more. But this business with you and Jet, we wouldn't have anticipated in a million years.'

'I should've. I've been having awful dreams, and even Jet said he had a feeling the bad things weren't over, in spite of Hettie saying they come in threes.'

'And this is the fourth?' Cathy asked.

'Yep.'

Christy got to her feet. 'Well, let's hope Hettie's wrong because if they do come in threes and this is the fourth, that means we've got another two bad things to go to make it six, or two lots of threes in other words. Oh. Do you think I've had too much wine to go and work behind a bar?'

'No.' Cathy stood up and twisted her friend around so that Christy faced the door, laughing as she did so. 'I've had the same amount as you and I couldn't have said that sentence. See you later. Have a good night.'

'Same to you,' Christy said. 'And don't worry, Mia, Jet will see the light and appear on his white charger to take you back. I'm sure of it.'

But he didn't, and by the time Christy got back at eleven-thirty, Mia and Cathy had started on the ice cream.

'I'm not sure if you want to hear this,' Christy said, slumping into a chair, kicking off her shoes and taking the bowl of ice cream Cathy handed her. 'Jet was in the pub.'

Mia's spoon hovered in the air, halfway between her mouth and the bowl. 'He was? Was he ... alone?'

Christy gave Cathy an odd look. 'He was talking to Alexia most of the night from what I could tell. We were pretty busy and she did come and help out from time to time, but mainly they were huddled in a corner, deep in conversation.'

'Huddled?' The spoon clanked against the bowl as it fell into it. 'What? Like they were ... together?'

Christy shrugged. 'Not exactly together, but they were ...'

'What?' Mia demanded.

'I wasn't sure if I should say this, but I think it's best you know the truth. They were pretty intense. And when Alexia was serving, I couldn't help but notice that Jet was staring at her. Just staring, you know, as if he had a great deal on his mind and most of it involved Alexia. But that doesn't mean there's anything going on. He could've been comparing her to you and thinking how daft he was to let you go and how wonderful you are.'

'Yes,' Mia said. 'Because Alexia isn't in the least bit beautiful, is she? She doesn't have the body of a goddess and hair any woman would die for and lips that any man would long to kiss and eyes that sparkle like the stars, and her laugh isn't the sweetest sound you'll ever hear and she doesn't play rugby, and isn't good with kids and … oh wait. She's all those things and more.' Mia grabbed the wine and topped up her glass.

Christy and Cathy exchanged looks.

'I don't think it's Garrick that Jet needs to be worried about,' Christy said, a hint of amusement in her voice. 'It sounds to me like you're in love with Alexia.'

'I hate her. Although she didn't tell Jet about me and Garrick kissing and she could've. I thought she had, but she hadn't. So she was also a good friend over that. Damn the bloody woman.'

'She may be beautiful,' Cathy agreed, 'and goodness knows I was worried when Leo first set eyes on her the other week, but as Leo said to me when I asked what he thought of her. "She's gorgeous, yes, but she's not you." And before you tell me that of course that's what he'd say, I believe him. You know why? Because Love doesn't worry about people's looks, or how good they are at sports or what they sound like. Love makes everyone look like the most gorgeous person on the planet to the person who Love makes them fall in love with.'

Christy laughed. 'We know what you mean, but you may be a bit too drunk to explain it properly.'

'It made perfect sense to me,' Mia said. 'Let's just hope that Love has made Jet see me as that person, and not Alexia. But if she thinks she can get Jet, she's got another think coming because I'm not going to give him up so easily. First thing tomorrow I'm going to go to Little Pond Farm and I'm going to have it out with him. I'm going to make him listen and understand what really happened. I'm going to make him love me again. Ella said I should make him realise what he might be losing, but I'm the one who's realised that. And I can't lose Jet. I really can't. Not even to someone as beautiful as Alexia.'

'Good for you,' Cathy said.

'Oh shit,' said Christy, screwing up her face. 'There's something else I haven't told you.'

'What?'

Christy took in a deep breath. 'As I was leaving the pub I saw Jet get up and ... well Alexia kissed him. There's no other way I can say it. She kissed him. Right there, in front of Toby and Bear and me and Freda and ... well, anyone who was still in the pub when it was closing.'

'She did what?' Cathy boomed.

Mia didn't say a word at first. She sipped her wine and stared at the floor. Eventually, she asked:

'And Jet? What did Jet do? Please don't tell me he put his arms around her and kissed her back. Please. Unless he did. Because you're right. I need to know the truth.'

'I'm not really sure. I saw them step apart after a couple of seconds, but whether that was her or whether he pushed her away I don't know because he had his back to me. I was so shocked. I don't know what happened after that because I had to get out of there. If I hadn't, I would've punched Alexia right in the face and as she's my boyfriend's sister, I really didn't want to do that. Although I think Toby was tempted to punch her himself. As he walked me home, all he kept saying was that he thought she'd changed but clearly she was playing games again and what a cow she was to do such a thing to you. Because she kissed Jet, I mean.'

Chapter Twenty-Two

Mia didn't get much sleep. Not because she had bad dreams, but because every time she closed her eyes she saw an image of Alexia and Jet locked in a passionate embrace. The only way to stop those images was to keep her eyes wide open. Even then, they managed to worm their way into her mind. She must've dozed off at some stage because she opened her eyes just as twilight was chasing away the darkness of the night, the silver glow, flicked with smudges of pink and grey, and pale red.

Jet would've been up for an hour or so. Unless …

No. He wouldn't have spent the night with Alexia. He wouldn't. They wouldn't still be snuggled beneath the duvet, kissing and cuddling and other things Mia couldn't bear to think about.

She wasn't the only one up. Daisy and Dylan were chattering and laughing downstairs. That meant Cathy would be up, even if Christy wasn't.

She showered and, using the towels Cathy had given her, quickly dried herself and dressed, dashing downstairs well before seven.

'Did you sleep?' Cathy asked, smiling as she handed Mia a mug of coffee.

'A little, I think. But not much.'

'Listen, Mia, about what Christy said last night. It may not mean anything at all. Everyone knows Jet loves you. I don't know him well, obviously and I've only just met Alexia but I can't see him choosing her over you. You're so different. Perhaps, in some small way, he was trying to get his own back by kissing her. You know. Now you're equal. That's strange, I know, and perhaps a little freaky, but men are odd sometimes.'

'I'll soon find out. I'm going to see him right now. If he still loves me, I don't care if he kissed Alexia last night. Provided that's all he did. But if he doesn't love me, I need to know so that I can decide where the hell I go from here. I never thought I'd have to plan a future without him. I don't know what that could be. The thought terrifies me. I'd have to move away from here because I couldn't bear to be so close and not to be with him. And it would kill me to see him fall in love with someone else. But if I have to face it, well, I have to.'

'It won't come to that, I'm sure. I'll keep everything crossed it goes well. Would you like some breakfast?'

Mia shook her head, gulped down her coffee and placed the empty mug on the counter. 'No thanks. I want to get this over with.'

Cathy hugged her. 'Good luck then. And whatever happens, if you need a place to stay, or a shoulder to cry on, or someone to get drunk and eat ice cream with, we're here for you. I know you've got Ella, but please feel free to come here anytime you want.'

'I appreciate that. Thank you. Bye girls.'

'Bye Mia.' To her surprise, both Daisy and Dylan jumped to their feet, ran to her and hugged her legs. Being small, they couldn't reach much higher.

'I needed that. Thank you.'

'You off?' Christy asked, tramping down the stairs as Cathy walked to the door with Mia.

'Morning. Yes. Off to face the tiger, or whatever the saying is. Thanks for last night, both of you.'

'Anytime. Wait.' Christy hurried to her and gave Mia a big hug. 'Give him hell, kid. And remember, he's lucky to have you, so don't think you need to compete with anyone. Good luck. Oh, do you need a lift? I'm probably still over the limit, but it's only a few metres really and no one's about at this time of day.'

Mia smiled. 'No thanks. The fresh air will do me good and help to clear my head. And as you say, it's not far. It'll only take fifteen minutes or so.' She threw her holdall on her shoulder, took a deep breath as Cathy opened the door, and headed down the drive of Corner Cottage.

She turned into the lane and let out a little scream as a car pulled up right in front of her. It almost knocked her over. While she steadied herself the driver got out and hurried towards her.

'Mia!'

'Jet? You nearly killed me. Or was that what you intended? What the hell are you doing?'

'I could ask you the same thing. Walking in the middle of the road when it's still dark out.'

'It's twilight. And I'm at the side of the road, not the middle.'

'It's … oh who gives a damn.' His voice had softened and his eyes shone with emotion. 'I love you Mia. I'm an idiot. A complete moron. An arse. And probably a lot more besides. I really do love you. Please forgive me for being such a jerk. Please come home. I'll do anything to make it up to you. Anything.'

'What?' She blinked several times. Had he really said that?

'Wait.' He looked concerned as his gaze took in her holdall. 'Where are you going? I thought you were staying here?'

'I was going to Little Pond Farm. To see you. To ask if you'll take me back. To ask if you'll forgive me.'

'You were?' His eyes lit up and a huge smile spread across his face. The sigh of relief was audible.

'I was.' She smiled too. Would things be all right?

A cloud came down as his smile faded. 'There's something I need to tell you first. Something that happened in the pub. But it wasn't what you might think.'

'Alexia kissed you. I know.'

Now he blinked. 'You do? And you were still going to come and ask me to take you back?'

She nodded. 'Yes, Jet. Because I love you. But I do need to know if you did anything else. And I know you'll tell me the truth because if you don't, you also know someone in this village will make sure I soon find out.'

He shook his head. 'I would never lie to you. If something happened I would tell you. But it didn't. That was it. And I didn't kiss her. Just like the thing with you and Garrick, Alexia kissed me.'

'And it took you a second or two to realise what was happening? Just like with me and Garrick?'

He nodded. 'Exactly like you and Garrick. But there's one more thing you should know.'

'Oh?' She held her breath.

'Alexia didn't kiss me because she wants me back. She really is falling in love with Garrick as I told you yesterday. She kissed me to prove a point. I know you don't think she's changed but she genuinely is back to the girl I grew up with – the true friend. I didn't want to go to the pub yesterday. I wanted to stay home and continue getting drunk. I was half cut when you left.'

'I thought you were. What were you saying about Alexia?'

'She insisted I meet her in the pub. She said she had something important to tell me concerning you. She knew I'd go if she said that. She spent the entire evening calling me a fool. She explained that it was Garrick who instigated the kiss between you two after you gave him a friendly peck on the cheek. According to what he told Alexia during their dinner, he hadn't really meant to. He told her he still has feelings for you but he's so mixed up since Fiona's death that he doesn't know what he's doing half the time. He said he simply got swept up in the whole Valentine's Day thing and the fact you'd had such a great afternoon. She told me one stupid little kiss didn't bother her so why should it bother me? And when I still couldn't see the wood for the trees and was adamant that you must've wanted him to kiss you, she kissed me in front of half the pub. I finally understood what you'd been trying to tell me. I stepped away from her and do you know what she said?' He laughed as he shook his head.

'No. What?'

'She said, "That's how two people can kiss when only one of them wants to, you bloody stupid pillock. Now do us all a favour and go and get your fiancée back, or I'll kick your arse from here to eternity and back again, you stubborn git."' He laughed harder. 'Alexia has always had a way with words.'

Mia was stunned. 'Alexia said that? Really?'

'Those exact words. I can remember every one. It's funny how, when you're trying to get drunk, you simply can't. I think I'd drunk myself sober. Honestly, ask Freda or Bear. They were both there. Toby had left but there were several others who can tell you that's precisely what she said. I would've come here last night, but although I could see the lights were on when I left the pub, I didn't want to ring the bell and wake the kids and I didn't think you'd be going anywhere last night. I didn't sleep a wink. I've been pacing the kitchen waiting until it was a reasonable time to call round.'

'I didn't get much sleep either.'

'Are you coming home, Mia? If you need more time, I'll understand. I'll wait for however long it takes.'

'I don't need any time. I told you. I was coming to ask you if you did.'

He shook his head. 'All I need is you.' He took the holdall from her and placed it on the bonnet of his car before gently easing her into his arms.

'And you're all I need, Jet Cross. You pillock.'

He grinned. 'I deserve that.'

She grabbed his jacket collar and pulled him closer. 'And I deserve this,' she said, kissing him.

'Morning, you two!' Glen tapped them on their shoulders just as they were easing apart. He was wearing his tracksuit and he jogged on the spot as he spoke. 'Sorry to interrupt but I assume this means you still want a date for your wedding and I got a cancellation last night. It's for this April. Is that too soon? Otherwise it's the dates I gave you yesterday morning, Jet.'

'April sounds good to me, assuming my gorgeous fiancée still wants to marry a jerk like me.' Jet pulled a pitiful face then smiled.

Mia smiled back. 'She does. But not in April.'

Jet frowned. 'What's wrong with April?'

'Nothing. But it's a cancellation and I remember what Hettie says about those. As much as I want to be your wife, I'd rather wait than tempt Fate, thanks all the same.'

'There was one date in May,' Glen said, 'And a couple in July, from memory. But I'll leave it up to you to choose. Sorry to disturb you. Glad it's all back on track though. Not that anyone believed it wouldn't be. See you later.'

'We'll take the May date,' Mia said, as Glen jogged a few steps away. 'I want to be Mrs Mia Cross as soon as possible. With the exception of the cancellation. I know neither Mum nor Ella has any plans in May. If others can't make it, I don't care now.

'Yes. The May date,' Jet repeated, nodding. 'Whatever day it is.'

'Right you are,' Glen said. 'I'll check the date, put it in the diary and send you a confirmation email.' He waved his hand and increased his pace as he jogged down Lily Pond Lane.

Mia smiled up at Jet and sighed. 'We've got a date for our wedding. Last night, I was worried there might not be one.'

Jet shook his head. 'Last night I was terrified there wouldn't. I'm such a jerk. I thought I'd got over that but clearly I still need some work.'

'We'd better get home.' Mia moved towards the car.

'Absolutely. Perhaps we could catch up on some sleep?' Jet winked at her as he held the door open, then grabbed the holdall, tossed it in the back and got into the driver's seat.

'Sleep? We don't have time to sleep. We've got a wedding to plan. These things don't plan themselves.'

He stared at her for a few seconds.

'What?' she asked. 'Are you having second thoughts?'

'Definitely not. But I've just realised two things. One is that the first time I saw you was last May. I was driving my tractor on Seaside Road and you were trying to get past.'

'Oh yes. But you were blocking the road, not driving along it. It seems like a lot longer than that, doesn't it? And the second thing?'

'That we've just had our first row since becoming a couple. Isn't it tradition to have make-up sex after a row?'

She grinned at him. 'Absolutely. But after that, we're planning our wedding.'

He started the car, put on his seat belt and, checking there wasn't another car in sight even though it was most unlikely there would be, made a two-point turn in the lane. 'That sounds like the perfect plan to me.' He drove to the stop sign at the end of Lily Pond Lane and turned onto Seaside Road, beaming like a Cheshire cat.

'And I know just who should be your best man.'

'You do?' Jet glanced across at her and smiled. 'Because it's really a toss-up between Toby and Bear, and possibly, Franklin. And I'm not sure I want to choose between them. Who do you think it should be?'

She nodded. 'I don't think you should have to choose between them. I think it should be Garrick Swann.'

He stomped on the brakes and stared at her, a stunned expression on his face, but his voice was calm, if a little apprehensive. 'Garrick? Are you serious?'

She turned in her seat, leaning over to kiss his cheek. 'Too soon for jokes?' She winked at him and grinned.

He relaxed visibly and grinned back, letting out a small sigh as he glanced in his rear-view mirror and turned on his hazard lights before pulling her towards him. 'Just a little, my darling fiancée. Just a little.'

Coming soon

A Wedding on Lily Pond Lane

The Angel Bell is ringing for Mia and Jet's Big Day – but will the Wedding of the Year go without a hitch?

Every bride wants the perfect wedding and Mia Ward is no exception. But she is the only bride in Little Pondale and everyone in the village has ideas for her Big Day. Drowning in suggestions, Mia needs some help.

When she bumps into childhood friend, Breanna Wright on a shopping trip to London, Mia's convinced it's Fate. Breanna's only ambition was to be a wedding planner with her own business, The Wright Wedding … so Mia doesn't hesitate.

Breanna's now got three months to plan a wedding where the sky's the limit, budget-wise. She should be over the moon. Especially as she'll get a chance to see old friends again, including her first love. There's just one tiny hitch ... Breanna doesn't have a wedding-planning business.

She should tell Mia there has been a slight mistake, but as usual Breanna's life isn't running smoothly and she could really use a break. And when you've dreamt about planning weddings all your life, how difficult can it be?

Will this be the chance Breanna's longed for? Or will Mia's Dream Wedding be Breanna's biggest disaster yet?

A Note from Emily

Thank you for reading this book. A little piece of my heart goes into all of my books and when I send them on their way, I really hope they bring a smile to someone's face. If this book made you smile, or gave you a few pleasant hours of relaxation, I'd love it if you would tell your friends.

I'd be really happy if you have a minute or two to post a review. Just a line will do, and a kind review makes such a difference to my day – to any author's day. Huge thanks to those of you who do so, and for your lovely comments and support on social media. Thank you.

A writer's life can be lonely at times. Sharing a virtual cup of coffee or a glass of wine, or exchanging a few friendly words on Facebook, Twitter or Instagram is so much fun.

You might like to join my Readers' Club by signing up for my newsletter. It's absolutely free, your email address is safe and won't be shared and I won't bombard you, I promise. You can enter competitions and enjoy some giveaways. In addition to that, there's my author page on Facebook and there's also a new Facebook group. You can chat with me and with other fans and get access to my book news, snippets from my daily life, early extracts from my books and lots more besides. Details are on the 'For You' page of my website. You'll find all my contact links in the Contact section following this.

I'm working on my next book right now. Let's see where my characters take us this time. Hope to chat with you soon.

To see details of my other books, please go to the books page on my website, or scan the QR code below to see all my books on Amazon.

Contact

If you want to be the first to hear Emily's news, find out about book releases, enter competitions and gain automatic entry into her Readers' Club, go to: https://www.emilyharvale.com and subscribe to her newsletter via the 'Sign me up' box. If you love Emily's books and want to chat with her and other fans, ask to join the exclusive Emily Harvale's Readers' Club Facebook group.

Or come and say 'Hello' on Facebook, Twitter and Instagram.

Contact Emily via social media:
www.twitter.com/emilyharvale
www.facebook.com/emilyharvalewriter
www.facebook.com/emilyharvale
www.instagram.com/emilyharvale

Or by email via the website:
www.emilyharvale.com

Printed in Great Britain
by Amazon